Violet's Turning Point

Violet's Turning Point

BOOK THREE

of the
*A Life of Faith:
Violet Travilla*
Series

Based on the characters created by
Martha Finley

MCP
Mission City Press

Franklin, Tennessee

Book Three of the *A Life of Faith: Violet Travilla* Series

Violet's Turning Point
Copyright © 2004, Mission City Press, Inc. All Rights Reserved.

Published by Mission City Press, Inc.

This book is based on the characters in the *Elsie Dinsmore* series written by Martha Finley and first published in 1868 by Dodd, Mead & Company.

Cover & Interior Design:	Richmond & Williams
Cover Photography:	Michelle Grisco Photography
Typesetting:	BookSetters

Unless otherwise indicated, all Scripture references are from the Holy Bible, New International Version (NIV). Copyright © 1973, 1978, 1984 by International Bible Society. Used by permission of Zondervan Publishing House, Grand Rapids, MI. All rights reserved.

Violet Travilla and *A Life of Faith* are trademarks of Mission City Press, Inc.

For more information, write to Mission City Press at P.O. Box 681913, Franklin, Tennessee 37068-1913, or visit our Web Site at:

www.alifeoffaith.com

Library of Congress Catalog Card Number: 2004106055
Finley, Martha
      Violet's Turning Point
      Book Three of the *A Life of Faith: Violet Travilla* Series
      ISBN: 1-928749-19-4

Printed in the United States of America
1 2 3 4 5 6 7 8 — 08 07 06 05 04

— FOREWORD —

*T*he summer that Violet Travilla turned sixteen, she lived an adventure that took her to Rome, Italy, and opened her eyes to the world beyond her comfortable life with her family at Ion plantation. Now, it is two years later, and Violet's commitment to serve God by serving others is about to be put to the test. In *Violet's Turning Point* — the third in the *A Life of Faith: Violet Travilla* series — Vi will visit New York City, and with the help of old friends and new, she will discover that serving others can be much more difficult than she ever imagined.

The character of Vi Travilla (and all the Dinsmore and Travilla family) was created in the nineteenth century by Miss Martha Finley, a schoolteacher who devoted the last half of her life to writing books of faith for Christian youth. Miss Finley understood that young people wanted and needed stories that applied timeless Christian values to the "modern" challenges they faced. A century and a half later, Miss Finley's inspirational themes remain as fresh and relevant to young Christians as they were in her era. And Mission City Press is proud to continue her commitment in the *A Life of Faith* books based on Miss Finley's unforgettable characters and stories.

With Violet Travilla, readers can experience what life was like in another age and share Vi's ongoing adventures as she faces choices that are not so very different from today's.

v

∾ A Brief History of New York City ∾

The New York City that Vi visits in 1881 would not have looked at all like the New York City of today for one immediately obvious reason—no skyscrapers! But it was already America's largest and most exciting city—a world capital of finance and commerce and a growing center of art, literature, and entertainment.

New York is also one of the country's oldest cities. From the beginning, its location attracted Europeans who saw its potential as a trade and shipping site. The long, narrow island of Manhattan (which most people think of as New York City) stretches roughly north to south between the Hudson River on the west and the Harlem and East Rivers on the east. The rivers flow directly into the Atlantic, providing a large, protected harbor for ocean-going ships.

Manhattan's original inhabitants were Native Americans of the Algonquin and Iroquois nations. The first Europeans arrived in 1524, when the Italian Giovanni da Verrazzano, who sailed for the French, entered the harbor and named it Santa Margarita. But it was the Dutch who settled there. Based on reports from Henry Hudson, an Englishman who explored the area in 1609, the Dutch West India Company established a trading post on the southern tip of the island. Colonists followed, and by 1626—when the island was "purchased" by Peter Minuit from the indigenous Manates Indian tribe—the colony of "New Amsterdam" was already an active center of commerce. Furs, grain, and other goods were brought down the Hudson River (named for the explorer) from New England and Canada and shipped on to markets in Europe. In addition to its busy harbor, colonial Manhattan soon boasted many farms. The middle and north-

ern parts of the island, where high-rise buildings stand today, were once fields of wheat and pastureland.

In 1664, New Amsterdam was surrendered by the Dutch to a British naval fleet sent to the area by the Duke of York, and the town was renamed New York. Despite the arrival of workers from many parts of Europe and the importation of African slaves, New York retained its distinctly Dutch and English character well into the nineteenth century.

From political rather than spiritual motives, the early Dutch governors instituted a policy of religious tolerance that was generally followed by the English. There were, however, periods of religious repression and racial conflict under both Dutch and British rule. Treatment of African-Americans during a thirty-year period in the early 1700s was particularly cruel. Problems also arose between the Dutch and British merchant families, who considered themselves the elite class, and working class immigrants who came from Europe and later, the Caribbean area and Asia. New York's tradition of ethnic and national diversity is almost as old as the city itself. As far back as 1643, a Catholic priest counted eighteen different languages being spoken in New Amsterdam.

By 1700, New York had a population of 5,000. (Today's Greater New York consists of five distinct counties called *boroughs*: Manhattan, Brooklyn, Queens, the Bronx, and Staten Island, which are home to more than eight million people.)

The island and the counties around it prospered in the first half of the 1700s, but the British rulers—who profited from this prosperity—tried to overload their colonists with taxes. The merchants of New York rebelled, and conflicts between local residents and British soldiers stationed in the city became routine. What many historians consider the first "battle" of the American Revolution took place in Manhattan — at Golden Hill, near what is now City Hall — six years before the Declaration of Independence.

When full-fledged war broke out in the summer of 1776, General George Washington immediately tried to secure New York's strategic harbor, but his army of colonists was unsuccessful in several battles, and New York was occupied by British forces. During seven years under British military control, the city's economy suffered and its population declined; two devastating fires destroyed most of the buildings from the colonial era.

The period after the war was much better for the city. Under the Articles of Confederation, it became the first capital of the United States. It was in New York that George Washington was inaugurated as President. The first meetings of the U.S. Congress and Supreme Court were held there. New York City also served as the state capital of New York until 1797. By 1800, New York was the largest city in the new United States, with a population of around 30,000 residents. That number doubled in just ten years — announcing a century of extraordinary growth.

The city's business still centered on its harbors. The completion of the Erie Canal in 1825 created a connection between the Great Lakes and the Hudson River. More canals were being built in states like Ohio and Indiana, and by the 1840s, goods could be shipped between New York and New Orleans completely by inland waterways. By the mid-1800s, more people and goods passed through the ports of New York than all other U.S. ports combined.

New York was also growing as a center of banking and finance, insurance, and manufacturing. The city's first commercial bank was founded in 1784 by Alexander

Foreword

Hamilton, and the New York Stock Exchange was organized in 1817. Wall Street (named for a wood fortification built by slaves during the Dutch colonial period) was the financial heart of the city. Great newspapers were founded, including Horace Greeley's *New York Tribune* (the country's leading anti-slavery voice) in 1841 and *The New York Times* in 1851. Book and magazine companies were established that would soon make New York the publishing center of the nation.

The New York that we know today was taking shape. In 1811, the city fathers adopted the grid plan for streets and blocks. Early in the 1840s, a public water and sewage system was begun with the construction of a huge water reservoir in what is now Midtown Manhattan. The farming areas to the north of the island began to give way to residential and commercial building.

Industry and manufacturing increased dramatically during the Civil War. Shipbuilding, which was always an important industry, now included the construction of naval battleships and freighters. The railroads supplied the Union armies with goods made in or shipped from the city. Despite the anti-draft riots of 1863 (during which New Yorkers directed their anger at the federal government's military conscription law against the city's African-American population, with tragic consequences including the lynchings of at least eighteen innocent men and the burning of an orphanage for African-American children), New York sent more soldiers to fight for the Union than any other city.

After the Civil War, the city and the nation boomed. Great fortunes were made in new industries and railroads, and optimism was limitless. But rapid, uncontrolled economic growth also led to widespread corruption in business

ix

and government. The collapse of one of New York's major financial firms in September 1873 caused panic and started one of the nation's worst economic depressions. The whole country—farmers in particular—suffered through four hard years, until the economy at last began to recover.

∾ NEW YORK IN THE 1880s ∾

By 1881, when Vi visits New York, the city was prospering again. It wasn't yet the "city of skyscrapers," but it was impressive. Building was going on everywhere, and New Yorkers were transfixed by the sight of the enormous bridge rising over the East River. When it opened in May of 1883, the Brooklyn Bridge was the longest suspension bridge in the world.

Another soaring monument, the Statue of Liberty, still lay in pieces around the city; visitors could climb inside the hand holding the torch, on display in Madison Square. The statue had been shipped from France in parts, but it could not be assembled until it had a pedestal. A fund to raise money to construct the base was started in 1884, and newspaper publisher Joseph Pulitzer urged his readers to contribute. With more than 120,000 donations (ranging from a few pennies to thousands of dollars), the pedestal was finally completed; Lady Liberty was officially opened in 1896.

In 1881, New York was still lit at night by gas lamps, but that was about to change. Financed by wealthy investors, Thomas Alva Edison built an electric light system in the Wall Street district. The first outdoor electric lighting began in September 1882. With the perfection of indoor incandescent lightbulbs, electricity soon brightened homes, stores, and offices throughout the city.

Foreword

New Yorkers in 1881 got around on foot, in horse-drawn carriages and carts, and by streetcar—buses pulled by horses along metal tracks. The first elevated, steam-powered railway opened in 1868, and by the time Vi visits the city, a traveler could ride the overhead train from the southern end of Manhattan to Central Park. The use of horses made street cleaning an endless task. But by the end of the century, streetcars would run on electricity, and work on the famous New York subways would be underway.

Another invention was already changing New York in 1881—the telephone. First demonstrated by Alexander Graham Bell at the 1876 Philadelphia Centennial, telephones were in limited use in New York just two years later. Phone service was expensive, so most early customers were businesses. But private phone service boomed when costs came down in the 1890s, and New York was on its way to becoming the nation's telecommunications center.

During her visit to the city, Vi is able to enjoy the natural splendor of Central Park—America's first landscaped city park. The site—two and a half miles long and a half-mile wide—was selected because its rocky terrain and swampy bogs were unsuitable for business and residential development. Designed by Frederick Law Olmstead and Calvert Vaux, the park was intended to look as natural as possible. The work was very difficult, because virtually everything that appears so natural, including the park's lakes, ice-skating ponds, large lawns, and wooded areas, had to be built and planted. Approximately forty-five million cubic feet of earth and rocks were moved, and more than a hundred miles of drainage pipes were laid. Cross streets were dug out below ground level. Although a small park section was opened in 1858—a year after construction began—the work continued for almost twenty years, with thousands of men laboring ten hours a day, six days a week, for wages of $6 to $9 a week.

Central Park quickly became a gathering place for the wealthy, who loved to parade their fine carriages and fine clothes for all to see. The city's poor and working classes lived too far away to walk to the park and couldn't afford the streetcar fares. It wasn't until around 1900 that the city began to offer park activities on Sundays—the only day that working people had to themselves.

Many of the descendants of the old Dutch and British merchant aristocracy continued to live in neighborhoods on the lower end of the island, but the city's new generation of wealthy capitalists were attracted to Central Park, and they began to build their homes around it. The best sites were on Fifth Avenue, which runs the length of the park.

Department store magnate Alexander Turney Stewart started the trend with his $3 million marble home completed in 1869. Not to be outdone, William Vanderbilt (then the richest man in the country) built *two* Fifth Avenue mansions in the early 1880s. Side by side, they spanned a city block and cost somewhere between $6 and $7 million. Such excessive displays of wealth led writer Mark Twain to call this period America's "Gilded Age."

Though commentators at the time said that such monumental "palaces" would stand forever, most of the homes along "mansion row" were eventually torn down. (A few remain. The Frick Collection, for example, is located in the former home of Henry Clay Frick, who made his fortune in steel. Today's visitor can see a superb collection of art, donated by Frick to the city, and get a taste of the lifestyle of New York's richest residents in Vi's time.)

Foreword

Many wealthy New Yorkers wanted their city to be a cultural center comparable to Paris, Rome, and London. So they contributed to the establishment of museums like the Metropolitan Museum of Art (opened in 1870) and the Museum of Natural History (opened in 1869); built fine libraries like the Astor Library; and supported New York's educational institutions including Columbia University (founded as King's College in 1754), New York University (1831), and Fordham University (1851).

Artists and writers from all parts of the country gravitated to New York: the Hudson River painters, poets like Walt Whitman, and writers including Herman Melville, Willa Cather, and O. Henry. Some of the most perceptive novels of upper class life were written by native New Yorkers Edith Wharton and Henry James. Music and theater thrived.

New York's international reputation as a fashion capital grew out of the clothing industry that, by 1910, employed almost half of all the city's workers. New Yorkers of the 1880s also loved sports—from college football games to horseracing, yachting in the harbor to swimming at Coney Island and the many other public and private beaches that lined the shores of the five city boroughs.

For those with enough money and leisure time—the upper and, to a lesser degree, the middle classes—New York in the 1880s was indeed the most fabulous city in America. But beneath the bright surface, there was a dark underside.

∞ POVERTY AND THE CITY ∞

The dazzling city was built through the labor of hundreds of thousands of people who were excluded from its

xiii

prosperity, and in *Violet's Turning Point*, Vi will be introduced to poverty of a kind she has never encountered before.

Between 1850 and 1900, almost seventeen million men, women, and children traveled across the oceans to the shores of the United States—the majority landing in New York, where their first stop was Castle Garden, the city's main immigration center before the opening of Ellis Island. They came mainly from impoverished rural areas of Europe. Many had just enough money to pay for their passage, the "head tax" collected on arrival, and perhaps a train ticket to their final destinations. Some brought little more than the clothes on their backs. But they almost all shared the dream of making better lives for themselves.

Fortunate immigrants had family in the United States, but the bulk were young men and women—often still in their teens—and young families who had to make their way alone in a new and strange land. Large numbers of immigrants traveled to the central and western regions of the nation, where they could acquire land, farm, start businesses, and participate in the settlement of the new territories. The majority, however, stayed near the eastern Atlantic coast, seeking work in industry and manufacturing. They crowded into the large cities—Chicago, Boston, Philadelphia, Pittsburgh, Cincinnati, and especially New York. By 1890, four of every five residents of the Greater New York area were either new immigrants or the children of immigrants. The cities also attracted many native-born Americans. Events such as the Depression of 1873 devastated many farms, and young people raised in rural communities flooded into the cities, looking for work and their share of the American Dream.

Foreword

New York and other urban areas were poorly prepared for so many new people, and there were almost no services to help immigrants adjust to their new country. Decent housing was nearly impossible to find in New York. Immigrants were crammed into tenement houses where whole families paid to live in one or two small, windowless rooms with no water or sewers. Sanitation and medical care were almost nonexistent. Tenement houses were stifling in the summer, bitterly cold in the winter, and always subject to outbreaks of deadly diseases like cholera, typhoid, yellow fever, and smallpox. Tuberculosis claimed thousands of victims. Fire was a constant threat, but means of escape were rarely provided. Crime was rampant, yet policing was scarce, and the poor lacked the power to demand protection or justice.

Many immigrants spoke little or no English, so they tended to live with people of their native nationality or ethnicity. Germans clustered with Germans, Irish with Irish, Italians with Italians, and so on. This ethnic heritage is reflected in the names of many New York neighborhoods today—Little Italy, Spanish Harlem, Chinatown.

Those who got jobs were usually relegated to the lowest and most poorly paid positions, working for twelve or more hours a day. Workplaces were dangerous, but few employers felt any obligation to protect their employees. There were no labor laws to regulate working hours, pay, and safety. Children under age thirteen were not supposed to be employed, but they often were. There was no such thing as medical insurance, and workers who were hurt on their jobs had to fend for themselves without any assistance.

It's a sad fact that the governments, including the police and law courts, of most large American cities in the second

half of the nineteenth century were corrupt. Politicians and wealthy industrialists often conspired against any efforts to improve working and living conditions for the poor. City housing for immigrants and poor Americans was generally owned by landlords who did nothing to provide the basics of decent living, though these owners had no scruples about collecting high rents.

Efforts at reform made some inroads, but laws designed to improve living and health standards were difficult to enforce. The obstacles to change also included widespread prejudice against the poor. Many Christian Americans accepted the notion that being poor was a moral failing. As Henry Ward Beecher, one of the most influential Protestant ministers of the time, once said, ". . . no man in this land suffers from poverty, unless it be more than his fault—unless it be his *sin*."

In the New York of the late nineteenth century, rich and poor were often separated by just a few city blocks, but it might as well have been an ocean. A journalist named Jacob August Riis, himself an immigrant from Denmark, took his camera into the slums of the Lower East Side—the city's poorest area—and documented the living conditions he had seen in his years as a police reporter. His book *How the Other Half Lives* (1890) horrified many good people, among them Theodore Roosevelt, who was then Police Commissioner of New York City. Riis had his own prejudices, but his book is regarded as one of the most important spurs to social reform ever written in the United States.

In *Violet's Turning Point*, Vi will see firsthand something of the conditions that Jacob Riis described. What she learns in the city will have a profound effect on her determination to live a life of faith and service.

Travilla/Dinsmore Family Tree

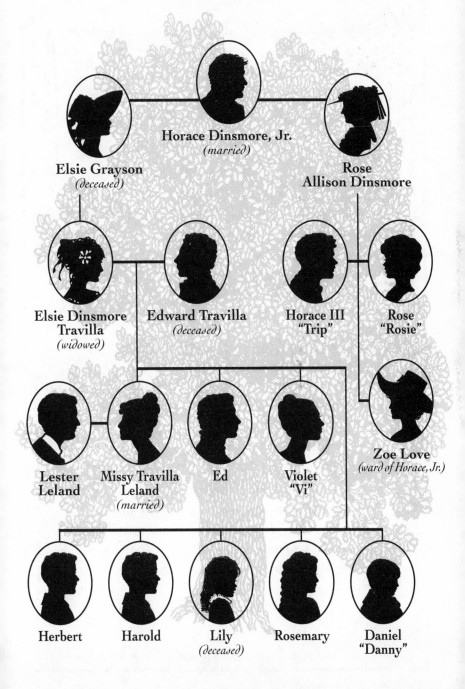

Horace Dinsmore, Jr.
(married)

Elsie Grayson
(deceased)

Rose
Allison Dinsmore

Elsie Dinsmore
Travilla
(widowed)

Edward Travilla
(deceased)

Horace III
"Trip"

Rose
"Rosie"

Lester
Leland

Missy Travilla
Leland
(married)

Ed

Violet
"Vi"

Zoe Love
(ward of Horace, Jr.)

Herbert

Harold

Lily
(deceased)

Rosemary

Daniel
"Danny"

SETTING

*T*he story opens in a university town in an Eastern state. It is early June 1881.

CHARACTERS

∞ ION ∞

Violet Travilla (Vi) — age 18, the third child of Elsie and the late Edward Travilla.

Elsie Dinsmore Travilla — Vi's mother; a wealthy widow and the owner of Ion, a large farming estate in the South, and other properties.

Elsie ("Missy") Travilla Leland — married to **Lester Leland**. They live in Rome, Italy.

Edward Travilla, Jr. (Ed) — age 22, Vi's elder brother; a student in his final year at a famous Eastern university.

Herbert and Harold Travilla — age 15, Vi's twin brothers.

Rosemary — age 10, Vi's younger sister.

Daniel ("Danny") — age 7, Vi's youngest brother.

∞ OTHERS ∞

Mrs. Maureen O'Flaherty — formerly housekeeper at Elsie Travilla's plantation in Louisiana and now Vi's travel companion and friend.

Zoe Love — age 16, the daughter of a American diplomat.

Mrs. Louise Dinsmore Conley — Vi's widowed great-aunt.

Virginia Conley Neuville — one of Louise's married daughters.

∞ NEW YORK CITY ∞

Mr. and Mrs. Despard — a well-to-do couple, friends of Ed Travilla.

Amelia Frazier — Mrs. Despard's sister.

Mrs. Maurice Vangelt — a member of New York's high society.

Mr. Phillips — Elsie Travilla's lawyer in New York, and an old family friend.

Monsieur Francois Alphonse — an art dealer from Paris, France.

Mr. Biggs — the business associate of Monsieur Alphonse.

Kevin Meriweather — a carriage driver.

Mrs. Giannelli — the mother of eight young children.

Mrs. Weaver — an elderly widow.

Sergeant Doyle — a policeman.

Signor Vivante — an Italian gentleman visiting New York.

CHAPTER

1

A Family Gathering

God sets the lonely in families.

PSALM 68:6

A Family Gathering

*Z*oe Love almost skipped into the sitting room of the small, pleasant apartment. The smile on her pretty face was so charming that it brightened even the somber black of her dress and the small black hat perched on her blonde hair.

She sank down next to Vi Travilla on the leather couch and declared, "Now I wish more than ever that I'd known your father! He surely must have been what my own Papa called 'a man of many parts'."

Vi smiled softly. "Yes, he was," she replied. "I sometimes think there was very little my father could not do. Or at least try to do. Yet he almost never called attention to himself. Until today, I knew very little about his scholastic record when he was a student here at the University."

"The Chancellor's tribute was excellent, don't you think?" said Ed Travilla, who entered the sitting room of his apartment just in time to catch his sister's words. Now in his last year as a student at the University, Ed had grown as handsome as his late father and namesake. And to Vi's amusement, her brother now sported a moustache, just as their father had in his student days.

Vi and Zoe both agreed that the tribute was very moving, and the three young people began to review the dedication service they had just attended.

The previous week had been a special one for the Travillas. They'd traveled north to the lovely college town to be the guests of the University. The occasion was the dedication of a new wing of the school's famous library — an addition built at the bequest of Edward Travilla and named in his honor. That morning, the family had attended

3

Violet's Turning Point

Sunday services at the University's chapel, followed by the formal dedication of the Edward Travilla Wing. The ceremony was the last of a lengthy schedule of events.

"I wonder what Papa would have made of all this," Vi said.

"I doubt there would have been much fuss if he were here," Ed said with a warm laugh. "Then again, Papa always loved a party, so he might have enjoyed himself thoroughly. I can't really say what he would have done."

"Can a child ever really know her parents?" Zoe asked, and Vi caught the melancholy note in her young friend's voice. It had been only a few months since Zoe had come to live in the United States after the death of her father, and the girl's loss was still as fresh as a new wound. Despite Zoe's sunny personality, her sadness would sometimes break through, and Vi—who had lost her own beloved father four years earlier—understood the pain.

Zoe lowered her eyes and continued, "I thought I knew everything about my Papa, but there are so many questions I would like to ask him now. Not big questions, but little things. Like what games he liked to play when he was a boy and what his favorite subjects were in school. Now I'll never know."

Vi laid her hand over her friend's and said, "But you may. There is much you can learn as time passes, just as Ed and I learned more about our father today. As God heals the pain of our loss, He opens our hearts to new understanding of ourselves and the ones who love us. At least, that's been my experience."

Zoe raised her head and asked, "Did you ever feel that you might forget your father?" There was urgency in her voice, and Vi saw worry in the girl's delicate, heart-shaped face.

"I did," Ed replied. "There was a time when I realized that I could no longer picture Papa clearly in my mind. When I tried, his image was always that of the portrait that hung in his bedroom—not the living, breathing person who was so much a part of every day of my life. It frightened me, and I felt as if I were losing him all over again."

As Ed talked, Vi saw the anxiety in Zoe's face change to something like amazement.

"That happened to you too?" Zoe said.

"I think it happens to many people when someone they love dies," Ed replied. "I think it's a natural part of God's healing gift. It is a way of softening our eyes' vision so that we can focus on what is in our hearts. I can't see Papa clearly now, but all that he taught me lives on inside me and strengthens me."

Vi squeezed Zoe's hand gently and said, "We can't tell you how you should feel, but we know that God is here for you. Lean on Him, and He will guide you through your sorrow."

Zoe's face lit with a smile, and she said, "Oh, He has done so much for me already. He guided me here—I mean, into your family. Papa was all the family I had for so long, and when he died, I couldn't imagine how I could go on. Yet God has provided for me, hasn't He?"

Zoe Love had followed a difficult path over the past five months. Her father, a retired American diplomat, had been ill for some time, but still his death nearly shattered his daughter. That had been in January, in Rome. Although Mr. Love left Zoe a considerable inheritance, she was not quite sixteen when he died and had no family of her own to turn to. Mr. Love's friends in Europe, where he had lived for more than thirty years, would have gladly taken Zoe in.

But her father's wish was that she go home to her native land, and his old friend Horace Dinsmore had pledged to fulfill that wish.

So Zoe, who had never before set foot on American soil, journeyed across the Atlantic Ocean and to the South and came into the Dinsmore and Travilla homes and hearts. Vi, who had met Zoe in Rome in the summer of 1879, welcomed the girl like a sister, and all the younger Travillas soon followed her lead.

Zoe actually lived with Vi's grandparents, Rose and Horace Dinsmore, at their plantation, The Oaks. But she spent almost as much time at the Travillas' neighboring estate, Ion. When this trip to the University was being arranged, Vi and Ed's mother had seen an opportunity to expand Zoe's knowledge of her country and invited the girl to join their party. It was an offer that Zoe accepted, as she did most things, with enthusiasm.

~~~~~

The young people soon turned their conversation to the Dinsmores. Vi expressed her disappointment that her grandparents had been unable to make the trip.

"Of course, Grandmamma shouldn't travel so soon after being ill," she said. "The influenza weakened her, and a trip like this would be too much for her until she has her strength back. And Grandpapa wouldn't leave her. Still, he'd have enjoyed being here, at his and Papa's old college."

"Your grandparents are so generous," Zoe observed. "I can't help wondering why Mr. Dinsmore is so willing to tutor me. I'm not the most attentive student, though he makes lessons much more interesting than any of my poor governesses ever did." She added with a small giggle, "I must have been a great trial to those ladies when I was a child."

Ed was about to comment that it was the student's responsibility to make the most of what was taught (for in his opinion, Zoe Love was still very much a child), but the sound of boys' laughter drifted through the open window and interrupted his thought.

Rising from his chair, Ed said, "That noise could only be the twins. Mamma's here."

Elsie Travilla and her sons Herbert and Harold were staying with the University Chancellor and his wife, while Vi, Zoe, and their chaperone, Mrs. O'Flaherty, were lodging at a hotel not far from Ed's apartment. The previous week had been so full of activities that the family had not had much time to visit with each other. Everyone was looking forward to this quiet Sunday afternoon together at Ed's apartment—actually the first floor of a quaint old house on a quiet street near the University campus.

The twins, now fifteen and almost as tall as their big brother, bounded like rambunctious puppies into the sitting room, followed more sedately by their mother.

"Where is Mrs. O'Flaherty?" Vi asked.

"She'll be here soon," Elsie said. "She wanted to stop at that little market up the street. She had some things to buy."

"Maybe some sweet cakes for our tea," Herbert added hopefully.

Elsie took her seat in a chair that had once been among the furnishings of her husband's library at Ion. Unconsciously, she rubbed her fingers lightly over a worn place on the wooden arm of the chair. When Ed had taken the apartment, Elsie had shipped a number of items to her son—including the chair, a desk, the bed that had been her husband's before they married, and several framed botanical engravings that Mr. Travilla had collected during his college days.

"I shall miss my visits here after you graduate," she said to Ed. Her gaze rose to the engravings hanging above the fireplace. "In this room, I can imagine what your father's life was like when he was a student."

"Didn't you know Mr. Travilla then?" Zoe asked.

"No, dear, for I was but a little child when he was in college," Elsie explained. "Mr. Travilla was a good deal older than I in years. But young in spirit always."

Zoe smiled softly and said, "My Papa was older than my Mamma, too."

At that point, Ed—who did not want Zoe to slip into her grief again—asked cheerfully, "Well, is everyone ready for our journeys tomorrow? Harold and Herbert, have you fellows packed up yet?"

The next morning, Elsie and the boys would travel home to the South. Harold and Herbert were especially anxious to see their little sister and brother (who, it had been decided, were still too young for the formal dedication ceremonies) and to begin another summer at Ion. But Elsie had arranged a special holiday for Vi and Zoe. The girls and Mrs. O'Flaherty were to spend the whole month of June in New York City. They were going to stay at a luxurious new hotel that overlooked Central Park, and Ed would accompany them to the city and remain there for a few days before returning to begin his summer classes. They would also be joined by Mrs. Louise Conley, the sister of Horace Dinsmore, who would be coming from her home at Roselands to visit her daughter.

Herbert and Harold asserted that they were "nearly" done with their packing, and Ed asked the same question of Vi and Zoe.

8

Vi laughed and replied, "Don't worry, big brother. We girls won't make you wait at the train station."

"I don't have much to pack anyway," Zoe said, "since I will be getting a new wardrobe in New York. It's been ever so long since I went shopping."

There was an edge of excitement in Zoe's voice that Elsie was glad to hear.

Elsie said, "Your father was a wise man to ask that you not wear mourning clothes for a minute longer than was proper. I'm sure you will enjoy shopping in New York. You have appointments with several of the best dressmakers there. I look forward to seeing you in summer colors when you come back to us in July."

"She should get some blue dresses," Harold piped up, "to match her eyes." An embarrassed flush came to his cheeks, and he looked to his twin in a pleading way.

But Herbert was no help at all. "Aw, you don't know anything about girls' clothes, Harry," he said, poking his brother's arm. "You'd think Zoe looked good in a grain sack."

It was Vi who came to Harold's rescue by adroitly shifting the subject. "I think blue is just Zoe's color," she said. "I remember that bonnet you wore, Zoe, when we were in Rome. The one that tied with the blue satin ribbon. It was so becoming. By the way, has anyone heard from Missy and Lester? Do they intend to stay in Rome this summer?"

"Thanks for reminding me, Vi. A letter from Missy came late last night," Ed answered. "It's addressed to the whole family." He went to his desk and began moving some papers about. "Here it is. I didn't want to open it until we were all together. Mamma, would you read it to us?"

He used a letter opener to slit the flap, then handed the thick envelope to his mother. She removed several sheets of white paper and began to read aloud what her eldest daughter had written from Rome, where Missy and Lester Leland had lived since their marriage.

My dear, dear family,

Lester and I wish so much that we could be with you to celebrate the dedication of the new library wing and be at your sides to honor Papa. It seems impossible that we haven't seen our families for almost two years. But I'm afraid ocean voyages will not be on our schedule for some time to come. I have such wonderful news — God has truly blessed us, and sometime early next November, we will be parents! Is there a greater joy in this world?

At these words, everyone save Elsie herself sent up gleeful cheers. Harold pounded Herbert's back and exclaimed, "We're going to be uncles, my boy!"

Vi asked her mother, "But did you know?"

"It's not totally a surprise," Elsie smiled. "I received a letter from Missy just before we left Ion, and I suspected we might be hearing this news before long." Then she held up her hand and said, "There's more. Shall I continue?"

There was a chorus of "Yes, please," and Elsie read on.

I am fine, and Dr. Di Marco promises to watch over me *come il falco* (that's "like a hawk" in Italian). Lester is ecstatic. The news has inspired him to begin a new series of portraits of children. And Vi, guess what? His first subjects are our darling Alberto and Angelina. The children send their love to you and Zoe, as does Signora Constanza. And please tell Mrs. O'Flaherty that we all miss her terribly.

A Family Gathering

The letter went on in this fashion, with personal messages to each family member and news of the Lelands' household in Rome. When Elsie finished reading, she suggested that they say a prayer of thanks for their loved ones abroad and the new life that God would soon bring into the world. They all joined hands, and Elsie spoke the words of joy and wonderment that were in their hearts.

A few minutes later, there was a knock at the door, and Mrs. O'Flaherty came in, her arms loaded with bags and boxes. The twins ran to take her packages and proclaim the news. Mrs. O'Flaherty's ruddy face glowed, and she beamed smiles on everyone—displaying her gold tooth. All conversation now turned to babies, and they wondered whether the expected addition to the family would be a boy or a girl. Then the subject of names was raised, and Harold asked if their new nephew or niece would have an Italian name. Zoe, who was fluent in Italian, suggested a few possibilities, and she and the twins quickly made a game of thinking up names.

Meanwhile, Mrs. O'Flaherty disappeared into Ed's small kitchen, and Vi followed. Together, they unpacked the shopping bags.

"That big brother of yours," Mrs. O'Flaherty said with a trace of womanly superiority. "He keeps his cupboards as bare as Mother Hubbard's, so I brought him some provisions. I was fortunate to find a market that was open on Sunday."

"I guess Ed dines out most of the time," Vi remarked as she stored containers of tea, coffee, crackers, tinned meats and fruits, and other basics in the little pantry.

"Well, he needs something here to keep himself nourished when he can't go out," Mrs. O'Flaherty declared firmly. "I've spoken to the lady who cleans for him. She's to see that his pantry remains stocked from now on."

"I'm so glad you're going to New York with us," Vi said as she removed a box tied with string from one of the shopping bags. She smiled, knowing that it contained the sweet treats that Herbert craved. "You take such good care of us."

"Of course, I do." Mrs. O'Flaherty laughed in her lilting Irish way. "And you, my dear Violet, make it easy for me. For you, I shall be only a proper chaperone. Zoe, on the other hand, will need all four of our eyes watching out for her. She's a wonderful girl, but a little too independent, I think, for New York."

"Do you think New York is dangerous?"

"It can be, if you don't know where to go and where not to go. Zoe knew Rome like the back of her little hand. But New York isn't Rome, and I fear she may be too confident of her ability to navigate its byways. All I'm saying, Vi girl, is that we must both be watchful. Zoe will be our responsibility. She's just sixteen, and that's an age when common sense can often be overcome by curiosity and an adventurous spirit. I should know."

Vi thought for a moment, remembering Mrs. O'Flaherty's stories of running away from her family and eloping with a penniless musician when she was still in her teens. Though Vi had no such worries about Zoe, she understood Mrs. O'Flaherty's concern.

"I'll do my part, Mrs. O," she said gravely. "I promise."

As twilight approached, Ed turned up the gaslights throughout the apartment, and the twins volunteered to help Vi and Mrs. O'Flaherty set the table for tea.

Zoe also offered to help, but Elsie asked her to take a walk in Ed's garden instead.

"I'll miss having you at Ion," Elsie said as they inspected a small patch of flowers planted in the side yard.

"You've been so good to me, Mrs. Travilla," Zoe replied. "I hope it's not too forward to say, but I feel as if I have a family now, with you and Mr. and Mrs. Dinsmore."

"What you say makes me very happy, for we think of you as family. Do you know that I also think you are very brave?"

"Me?" Zoe said in surprise.

"To come across the ocean and travel to a strange place and make your home with strange people. You knew my father and Vi, but you had not seen them for a long time, and you had no idea what the rest of us would be like," Elsie said compassionately.

"But it was because of Vi and Mr. Dinsmore that I didn't doubt Papa's decision," Zoe explained. "And Missy and Lester, who were so kind to me all the time Papa was ill. I had heard so many stories about your family and Ion and the South. Long before I came, I really felt as if I knew you."

"Still, it could not have been easy for you to leave Rome," Elsie said.

"It wasn't," Zoe admitted. "Europe was always my home, and I believed America to be a rough and wild place. But what really scared me was leaving my father. Oh, I know that he isn't really in Rome, that he's with God now, but somehow it felt like I was leaving him behind. I wasn't at all brave, Mrs. Travilla. I never told anyone this before, but I was afraid of the ocean. It seemed so big and deep and dangerous. If Mrs. O'Flaherty hadn't made the voyage with me, I could never have set foot on that ship."

Violet's Turning Point

Elsie laid her arm around Zoe's shoulder, realizing once again how young this lovely girl was. "But you did make the voyage," she said, "and that was an act of courage. Now, I want you to enjoy your holiday in New York. It will be fun for you to shop, but I hope you will see more of the city than just stores and dressmakers. Your father earnestly wanted you to learn about your country, and New York is a good place to begin. There are a great many worthwhile things to see and do there. Mrs. O'Flaherty knows the city well and will be an excellent guide. Vi, too, for she has visited New York a number of times. But I trust you both to be guided by Mrs. O'Flaherty as you would by me."

Zoe looked up into Elsie's face, and even in the shadows, Elsie could see the brightness in the girl's eyes. "Oh, Mrs. Travilla, you can trust me. And Vi, of course, because she is ever so much more grown up now that she's eighteen."

Elsie laughed sweetly. "I do trust you both, dear. But I am a mother, and it's my duty to give advice and issue warnings to my children, even the almost grown-up ones like you and Vi. Now then, I have one more request of you."

"Anything," Zoe said instantly, for at that moment, warmed by the thrill of being included among Elsie's children, she would have agreed to almost anything this loving and wise woman asked of her.

"It's high time you called me something other than 'Mrs. Travilla,'" Elsie said. "I propose 'Cousin Elsie' if that suits you. Though we aren't really cousins, we are family. So what do you think? May I be your Cousin Elsie?"

"Oh, that's so kind of you, Mrs.—ah—Cousin Elsie," Zoe said happily. "It's just ever so perfectly kind of you."

CHAPTER

Out and About in New York

*Let your conversation be always
full of grace, seasoned with
salt, so that you may
know how to answer
everyone.*

COLOSSIANS 4:6

Out and About in New York

*V*i and Zoe were standing at the open window of Vi's prettily decorated bedroom in the hotel. They looked out at the great park on the opposite side of the avenue. The sun was near setting, and the street bustled with carriages and streetcars filled with people hurrying home at the end of the workday. A cacophony of sounds rose to their ears, and from their third-floor observation point, the girls tried to catch words from the jumble of voices coming from the sidewalk below.

It was their second day in New York, and they too had been at work. At least it seemed like work to Vi, who had never much enjoyed shopping. After their breakfast, the girls and Mrs. O'Flaherty had been driven to the city's fashionable shopping area on Broadway. They'd visited a half dozen shops to discuss Zoe's new wardrobe with the skilled dressmakers who gowned the city's most elite clientele. They studied fabrics and design books until Vi's neck ached and her dark eyes burned. But Zoe's energy never flagged. Each new bolt of colorful silk and satin that was laid before her brought a fresh wave of excitement. She simply could not understand when Vi at last complained of fatigue and Mrs. O'Flaherty jokingly demanded to return to the hotel before her feet fell "as flat as corncakes."

Once back in their large, elegant suite, Mrs. O'Flaherty excused herself to take a nap. The girls read and chatted until it was time to dress, for they and Ed were to be treated to dinner that night.

"There are many beautiful parks in Rome," Zoe was saying, "but I don't think any are as large as this. Perhaps there are, but they don't look like this. This is like a sea of trees, a green ocean set right in the middle of the city."

"My Papa used to say how amazing it was that a city crowded onto a tiny island would devote so much space to trees and lawn and fountains," Vi noted. She thumbed through a small guidebook she'd purchased the day before. Finding the page she wanted, she read quickly, "It says that Central Park is almost 850 acres in size. The land was bought before the Civil War, and it took more than twenty years to complete the park. There are many other parks in the city, but none of this size."

"Is that very large?" Zoe asked. Then she giggled. "Oh, that did sound daft of me. But I've always lived in cities, and I never think of things like acres. I cannot imagine how big an acre is."

Vi smiled and said, "Well, I'm a farm girl, and I can tell you that an acre is exactly 43,560 square feet. And this bedroom is . . ." Vi looked around her and estimated the room's dimensions, then went on, "about 150 square feet. So one acre would be equal to nearly three hundred rooms like this one."

Open-mouthed with astonishment, Zoe stared at Vi as if she were a princess of Arabia or an empress of China who had just popped out of the woodwork. "H—how," she stammered, "how did you do that? How did you work out those numbers in your head?"

Vi grinned and said, "It's just an estimate. Papa taught me how to make educated guesses, so I could look at a field and estimate its area and the size of the crop it would produce. When you grow up on a farm, you just learn how to take the measure of things."

Zoe cocked her head to one side and looked into Vi's face with a serious expression. "Well, I cannot so easily take the measure of you," she said. "You are always surprising me with what you know and how you think. From the first time we met, I knew you were no ordinary girl."

"I hope that's a good thing," Vi said.

Zoe's serious expression was quickly rearranged by an impish smile. "Oh, it is!" she declared. "It's why I hoped so much to be your friend. And now we are friends."

"The very best of friends," Vi agreed happily.

The noise from the street faded as daylight turned to dusk and the park was cloaked in shadow. Moving away from the window, Zoe sat down on Vi's bed and said, "It will be nice to meet Ed's friends tonight. Do you know where we will be dining? It was ever so kind of Ed to invite me along. I know that he thinks of me as a silly child."

Vi was surprised by this remark. She realized that Ed had not been as warm to Zoe as were the rest of their brothers and sisters, but she didn't believe that her brother had betrayed his feelings to Zoe.

"Why do you think that?" Vi asked.

"Oh, it's clear to me," Zoe replied offhandedly. "I'm not criticizing him. When I'm twenty-two, I will probably treat sixteen-year-olds just the same way. You know—courteously but disinterested. It's natural, I think."

Vi's first instinct was to defend her brother, but Zoe hadn't complained of any offense. So Vi simply asked, "Does his attitude bother you?"

"Oh, no, not at all!" Zoe exclaimed. "I understand that young men do not like to be reminded of how close they still are to being children. When my Papa was in the diplomatic service, I saw how the young men who worked as secretaries and clerks at the embassies were always so proud and worked so hard to be sophisticated. They ignored me as much as they could, but it was not because of anything I did. Papa explained how they were just not as interested in children as they would be when they married and became fathers. Papa would probably say that Ed is just being his age. And that's why I truly think him very nice to invite me to dinner with you and his friends."

Vi suppressed a smile. She went to the dressing table and picked up her hairbrush. *I wonder who is really the more sophisticated,* she thought to herself as she transformed her thick, straight hair into a fashionable upswept style. *Is it my brother or my observant little friend?*

But she didn't voice her speculation. Instead, she said, "We're going to Domenici's. It's very famous. My guidebook says that it was started as a bakery but became the favorite dining spot for the city's wealthy and famous."

Another question came to Zoe, and she said, "Tell me again the names of the people we will be with. I must remember the names. Papa taught me that it makes people happy when you know their names. He said that 'Zoe' is a good name for remembering because it's short and a bit unusual. There are so few words that start with *z* that they're just naturally memorable—like 'zebra' and 'Zanzibar.' "

Vi had to think for a moment before replying, "Our hosts are Mr. and Mrs. Despard. His name is Christopher, and she is Marguerite. Mr. Despard went to the University, and that's where Ed met him. But he's a good deal older. About thirty, I think. He's in some kind of financial business, and Mrs. Despard is quite wealthy in her own right. Her sister will also be with us tonight. She's Miss Frazier. Ed doesn't know much about her, except that she's a suffragette."

"What's that?" Zoe asked.

"It means she is a supporter of the right of women to vote—to get the suffrage," Vi explained.

"Why should a woman want to vote?" Zoe inquired curiously. "Politics is so awfully boring."

Vi, who did not know very much about the cause of the suffrage movement, tried to explain, "Well, it's about having equal rights. Have you ever read the Declaration of Independence?"

Zoe shook her head. "No, but I know what it is. It's the letter that the Americans sent to the King of England when they wanted to be free."

Vi turned to look at her friend, and her eyes were intensely bright. "It's an amazing document," she said. "The founders wanted to state the reasons why they were ready to fight for their freedom from British rule." Carefully she quoted, "'We hold these truths to be self-evident, that all men are created equal, that they are endowed by their Creator with certain unalienable Rights, that among these, are Life, Liberty, and the pursuit of Happiness.'"

"It says all *men*," Zoe remarked a bit smugly. "Not men and women."

Vi agreed: "It does, but I think the suffragettes would say that it means all *people*. Just the way we mean all people when we use the word 'mankind.' Oh, I'm not really sure what they would say, but maybe Miss Frazier can tell us. I'm very interested to meet her."

Zoe crossed to the dressing table, and both girls looked at their reflections in the mirror. They made a study in contrasts. Vi was tall, slim, and dark-haired. Her face was not beautiful in a classic way, but very pretty. Her large brown eyes fringed with thick black lashes were riveting. They seemed to drink in everything and reflect back under-standing that was, indeed, extraordinary for a young lady of just eighteen. Zoe was at least six inches shorter than Vi. Her blonde hair curled about her face, kissing her pink cheeks. Her blue eyes verged on green and always seemed to be dancing with some secret delight. Despite her diminutive size and small frame, however, Zoe was not fragile; anyone who looked closely was sure to see the strength in the set of her small chin and the straight line of her shoulders.

"Well, I hope this suffragette person won't talk about politics all night," Zoe said as she pinched her cheeks to heighten their color. "That's the one bad part of being a diplomat's daughter. I always had to listen to grown people talking about politics," she said with a comical little pout.

She brushed at the skirt of her black dress and adjusted the lace at its collar.

"I wish I had one of my new dresses tonight," she lamented. "A beautiful dress of that silver blue silk we saw today. I had much rather make my first appearance at the famous Domenici's as a bluebird than as a dreary old crow."

Vi had to laugh. "Black dress or not, Zoe, you will never, *never* be dreary. Are you ready? Then let's go to the parlor. Ed may think we are both silly children, but we will show him that we are punctual ones."

The girls were suitably impressed by the glittering scene that greeted them at the restaurant. The main dining room of Domenici's was filled with elegantly dressed women and men smartly attired in evening clothes and white ties. A few of the women appeared a shade too bright, and their diamonds just a little too large. But there was an air of self-confidence about most of the diners that appealed to Vi. These people seemed born to their fine clothes and dazzling jewels.

The room was certainly noisy with conversation and laughter, but the sound was, to Vi's ear, harmonious, as if everyone had been trained not to offend when they spoke. Then she heard music — a band playing somewhere — and she thought that its tune was not meant to be distinct but to blend with the voices of the diners and the tinkling of silverware and crystal glasses.

Ed had given the names of his friends to the maitre d', who supervised the dining room. Immediately, they were led to a table at the far side of the dining room, where the Despards and Miss Frazier were waiting. Ed made the introductions; then he held Zoe's chair while Mr. Despard seated Vi.

Mrs. Despard was a lovely, willowy woman with auburn hair and pale skin. Vi guessed her to be a few years younger than her husband. Miss Frazier looked like her sister, though her fair complexion was tanned by the sun and no powder concealed her natural crop of freckles. Mrs. Despard wore a green satin gown cut to flatter her long neck and slim shoulders. Several strands of pearls joined with a diamond clasp encircled her throat. Her sister, on the other hand, wore a plain, brown linen suit and a simple white blouse. Her hair was pulled straight back and gathered in a knot at the back. Her only adornment was a small watch on her wrist. She smiled in a friendly way but seemed content to let her sister carry on the chitchat that always starts a meeting with strangers.

As soon as all were seated, Mrs. Despard leaned forward and told Vi and Zoe how very pleased she was that they could come. Then she asked, "Has Ed told you how he and Mr. Despard first met?"

Vi replied that she understood they'd met at the University.

"They did," said Mrs. Despard, "and it is a most interesting story. My husband belonged to several clubs when he was at school and one was an equestrian club. Then a couple of years ago, Chris—Mr. Despard—was invited to be a judge for the club's annual horse show. Well, guess who won Best of Show? It was your brother and that magnificent steed he brought up from your home in the South. Chris and Ed met at the celebration dinner that night, and they've been fast friends ever since. We've been hoping that Ed might come to New York to live after his graduation."

She glanced at Ed, who was in conversation with Mr. Despard, and then confided in a whisper, "Your brother would certainly be welcomed here, especially by all the marriageable young ladies in our crowd."

She laughed—a tinkling, girlish laugh. And Vi laughed too.

"It's hard for me to picture my brother pursued by the young ladies of New York," Vi said.

"That's because he's your brother," Mrs. Despard commented sagely.

She said apologetically that their table was not in the best position, but she had requested it because it was quieter than in the center of the room, and she valued good conversation above "being seen." The food, she added, was simply wonderful, and she hoped the girls were hungry.

There were waiters fluttering everywhere about the room; their swift movements made Vi think of butterflies

that would occasionally land at a table to deposit plates or fill glasses and then fly off to some other chore. A waiter appeared at the Despard table and laid menus before everyone, and then Mr. Despard addressed his guests.

"Please, choose whatever you like," he said affably. "This is a special evening for Marguerite and me. To be surrounded by old friends and new is one of life's great pleasures. And the night is made even better by the presence of my dear sister-in-law"—he nodded at Miss Frazier and smiled—"who can rarely spare the time for dining out. So let us eat and be merry tonight."

They turned to their menus, and after some minutes of concentrated study, they were all ready to tell Mr. Despard what they had selected. Mr. Despard made several recommendations to the girls, but when Zoe chose escargots for her first course, her host took exception.

"Escargots?" Mr. Despard questioned. "Are you sure that is what you want? I think you might prefer the shrimp or perhaps the grilled trout."

"The escargots will be fine for me, Mr. Despard," Zoe said politely.

"But do you know what it is?" Mr. Despard asked.

Zoe looked at him with a puzzled expression that Mr. Despard interpreted as meaning that she did not know. In fact, Zoe was puzzled by his question, for she knew exactly what she wanted.

Ed joined in impatiently, "Have the trout, Zoe. It's fresh from streams just north of here."

"Are the escargots not fresh?" Zoe asked him.

"Of course, they're fresh," Ed replied shortly. "This is the finest restaurant in New York. Chris just thinks you won't like the escargots."

Violet's Turning Point

"Why ever not?" Zoe wondered. She had no intention of causing a problem, but she could not understand why the men were so concerned. Hadn't she been told to choose what she wanted? And she wanted escargots.

Ed leaned toward Zoe and almost hissed at her, "Because escargots are *snails* — cooked snails."

Zoe thought Ed looked quite funny. His face was flushed, and there were two red dots on his cheeks.

"Well, I hope they are cooked," Zoe giggled. "The menu says 'escargots provincal.' That means snails in the French country way, cooked in butter and herbs. It is a most delicious dish. You should try it, Ed."

Ed sat back heavily in his chair and said nothing else. But Vi could see that he was angry.

The exchange ended when Miss Frazier said to her brother-in-law, "I would also like the escargots, Chris. I haven't eaten them since I was a student in Paris, and the taste will bring back fond memories."

The moment passed, and conversation resumed as Chris Despard gave their orders to the waiter. But Vi continued to observe her brother. His natural color had returned, and he was talking pleasantly with Mrs. Despard. Still, Vi wondered to herself, *What has Zoe done to annoy him so?*

Dinner proceeded without further incident. The food was excellent, and the conversation even better — especially when Vi discovered that Miss Frazier was actually *Dr. Frazier*, a physician with her own medical practice.

"My cousins Arthur and Dick are doctors," Vi said. "They both trained in Philadelphia."

"As did I," Dr. Frazier said, "though we would not have been at the same college. Women are still not allowed to train with men. After medical college, I studied for a year in Paris, assisting in research."

Vi was fascinated and asked more about Dr. Frazier's work. She learned that the doctor had worked primarily among the poor in Paris, trying to unravel the causes of diseases like diphtheria and cholera that so often swept through the ghettos of poverty in all great cities.

"And do you continue to do research?" Vi asked.

"In my small way," the doctor replied, "but when I returned to New York, I decided that my life's work was to treat disease. I opened a clinic here, and my patients are primarily mothers and children. Few men will seek help from a woman doctor," she added with a small, wry smile. "But perhaps that will change someday."

"Where is your clinic?" Vi asked. "Is it near?"

Mrs. Despard, who had been listening to her sister and Vi, said, "Amelia's clinic is not very far from here, but it might as well be on the other side of the moon."

"It is in one of the poorer areas," Dr. Frazier explained, "but there are worse places, Marguerite. You see, Violet, this city is something like a slice of onion. The poorest people live in the outer rings, and as you peel away the layers, you reach the middle class—the shopkeepers and bookkeepers and public employees. The wealthy live in the smallest ring at the center. Most of the people in this room have no contact with the poor except as servants and know nothing of the desperation of their lives. Yet hundreds of thousands of people, like the waiters who are making our evening so pleasant, will go home tonight to dwellings where a dozen or more people live in two small, dark, and airless rooms.

Violet's Turning Point

Unlike us, many of them will go to sleep without more than a piece of bread to fill their stomachs."

"Amelia, you make it seem as if no one cares," Mrs. Despard said. "You know that the city is doing everything possible to improve those dreadful conditions. But it takes time."

Dr. Frazier smiled gently and laid her hand over her sister's. "You're right, Marguerite," she said. "Some people care and there are a few signs of progress. But I shall not spoil this nice evening with my complaints. Why don't you tell us about your project?"

As Mrs. Despard began to describe her work for the city's new museum, Vi realized that Mrs. Despard, too, was a woman of intelligence and diligence. Her interest was art, and in raising the cultural standards of the city. Zoe joined the conversation at this point, and she and Mrs. Despard were soon discussing the great museums of Europe. Zoe began telling about one of the Grecian statues recently installed in the Louvre in Paris. In order to describe the statue's pose, she raised her arm above and behind her head in a graceful arc.

At just that moment, a waiter was passing behind her — a tray of glasses balanced on the palm of his hand. Zoe's hand struck his arm, and just for a fraction of a second, the startled man lost his concentration. The tray wobbled, the glasses trembled, and in spite of the waiter's efforts, everything fell to the floor with a crash.

The waiter began to apologize profusely, and several of his colleagues rushed to help clear away the broken glass. Meanwhile, Zoe was making her own apologies. In her confusion and embarrassment, she mixed Italian, French, and English phrases. Dr. Frazier, who sat next to Zoe, grasped the girl's hand and spoke in a low, soothing voice, "It's all right, dear. It was an accident. Only an accident. There is no fault."

"But will the man be in trouble?" Zoe asked as tears gathered in her eyes. "Will he lose his job? That happens, I know. And it was my fault."

Mr. Despard had risen and come to Zoe's side. "Nothing will happen to the waiter," he assured her. "I will explain to the maitre d' and make it clear that the waiter is not to blame." Then he smiled, and to Zoe, he suddenly seemed like a knight coming to her rescue. "Nor are you at fault, my dear," he continued, "for as Amelia said, it was only an accident. A few glasses were broken, that is all, and fortunately they were empty. See, everything has been cleared away. Everything is back to normal now."

Zoe wiped quickly at her eyes and said, "*Merci*—I mean, thank you very much, Mr. Despard. I feel so foolish and clumsy."

"Well, you mustn't," he said. "Accidents happen to everyone. Besides, we have not yet had our dessert, and I want you in a good mood so you can enjoy Domenici's famous chocolate cake. Will you allow me to order it for you?"

"Yes, sir," Zoe replied with gratitude. "I would be pleased if you order for me."

Chris Despard returned to his chair, and it seemed as if nothing had occurred. Plates were cleared, dessert ordered, and conversations were resumed. But Vi was conscious of one change, when she caught her brother staring at Zoe. There was a hard look in Ed's eyes—a hard and judgmental look that she had never seen before.

"She is the most exasperating child!" Ed was declaring as he walked the floor of his room. "I never should have suggested that the Despards include her for dinner."

"But you did, and it was the right thing to do," Vi said.

They had arrived back at the hotel just after eleven o'clock, and Zoe had gone straight to her room. When Vi peeked in a quarter of an hour later, she found Zoe sound asleep. So before retiring herself, Vi decided to go to her brother's room, which was at the opposite end of the hallway, and thank him for the evening.

But Ed was not in a mood to be thanked. He was still fuming, and he instantly made it clear that the cause was Zoe.

"Hardly the right thing," Ed replied sarcastically. "It was bad enough when she argued with Chris about the menu. Then spilling that tray. And talking with Marguerite about art? When Marguerite is truly an expert! Even the twins would have had the good sense to be seen and not heard on an occasion like this."

Vi was amazed at her brother's condemnations. She straightened her shoulders and determined to speak rationally, but she couldn't let Ed's charges go unchallenged.

"In the first place, she didn't argue with Mr. Despard. She was told to choose whatever she wanted to eat and she did. The tray was purely an accident that could happen to anyone, and Mr. Despard was very gracious about it. In fact, he was sweet in a way that reminded me of Papa. And as for talking art with Mrs. Despard—they both enjoyed the discussion immensely. I think Mrs. Despard was really taken with Zoe."

"I doubt that," Ed snapped.

"Well, she invited us to tea on Friday, and as we were leaving the restaurant, she also suggested that Zoe and I spend an afternoon at the museum with her next week."

Ed stopped his pacing and spoke in a calmer voice: "I imagine Marguerite was just being kind. She wanted to invite you and knew that Zoe was your responsibility. She was merely being hospitable to your guest."

Vi rolled her eyes upward and said, "That is simply not the case. If you'd been paying attention instead of getting angry, you'd have seen how much both the Despards liked Zoe. And Dr. Frazier did too."

Ed sank down on his bed and let out a deep sigh. "Are you sure of that?"

"Oh, Ed, I wouldn't say it if I weren't sure. I know that Zoe can be talkative, but she is never flighty or dull. She's lived an amazing life for a girl her age, and she's very clever. Why are you so hard on her? I've seen how sympathetic you can be. Remember how you talked with her about her father?"

"That was different," he said. "I know how it feels to lose one's father."

Vi smiled warmly at her brother and said in a teasing tone, "You also know how it feels to be sixteen, though perhaps you need to refresh your memory. I'm your little sister, and it is usually I who comes to you for advice. But I have some for you now. Eddie, you need to look into your heart and take this to the Lord. I cannot guess the cause of your—ah—your negative feelings, but I know that Zoe doesn't deserve them. Maybe there's something else on your mind. And you know as well as I do that there is One who will understand. All you have to do is ask Him, and He will hear you."

Ed ran his hand through his curly black hair and sighed again, but softer this time. "Of course you're right, my wise little sister. She's just a child, and I shouldn't expect so much of her."

Vi rose from her chair and saw Ed's Bible on the desk. She picked it up and went to him, laying a hand on his shoulder. She held out the Bible with her other hand and said, "Here's the place to start, Eddie dear."

He took the book and raised his face to Vi. He was looking a little sheepish now as he said, "I didn't even think to ask if you had a good time."

"Oh, I did, a splendid time," Vi enthused. She told him how much she liked his friends and how impressed she was by Dr. Frazier. They talked more, and Vi sensed that Ed was reconsidering his harshness toward Zoe. But Vi soon found herself trying to cover a yawn and knew it was time for her to go to her prayers and her bed.

"Will you join us for breakfast?" she asked as she was leaving. "Say, about nine, so we can sleep in for an extra hour. We girls are going to the dressmakers at eleven, and then Aunt Louise arrives tomorrow afternoon and . . ."

"And we'll all need our strength for that," Ed said, finishing his sister's sentence with a laugh. Then he added, "Thanks again for the advice, Vi, but will you do me a favor?"

"What?" she asked, hoping that whatever her brother wanted, it could wait until the next day.

He grinned, stroked his new moustache, and said, "Just don't call me 'Eddie' again, please. Not ever."

CHAPTER

Aunt Louise

They are darkened in their understanding
and separated from the life of God
because of the ignorance that is in
them due to the hardening of
their hearts.

EPHESIANS 4:18

Aunt Louise

At about the time that Vi, Ed, Zoe, and Mrs. O'Flaherty were sitting down to breakfast in the hotel dining room, a train was speeding northward toward New York. A middle-aged woman dressed in gray sat primly in a private compartment and seemed to be staring out the window, but in fact, her eyes barely registered the farmlands and small towns that hurried past.

She should have been an attractive woman. She was trim in build, with thick brown hair that showed only a hint of gray. For a woman in her early fifties, she had amazingly clear skin. Her eyes and arched brows were well shaped, as was her narrow nose. But her mouth—there was a hardness about her mouth that affected her entire appearance. It was a mouth that rarely smiled with pleasure. Her lips always seemed stretched thin in a disapproving line.

The strange thing was that Louise Dinsmore Conley had been a laughing girl. Growing up at Roselands, her father's plantation, she'd been a happy, playful little girl. She was a good student, though not as dedicated as she should have been and somewhat spoiled like all the Dinsmore children. But she was a cheerful companion to her many brothers and sisters. Eventually, she'd married a man she loved deeply. They moved to a fine plantation in Kentucky, and in the years before the Civil War, the Conleys had five children—three boys and two girls—whom they raised with love and perhaps too much pampering.

But the war came, and Kentucky was one of its earliest battlegrounds. Mr. Conley, an ardent Confederate, had signed up for service immediately. When he was killed in battle and then the plantation was burned and the land seized, Louise's heart turned to ice. With everything the Conleys owned taken away, Louise and the children were forced to return to her parents at Roselands. Before the war ended, Louise lost two of her brothers and her mother, and Roselands itself was all but destroyed. With each new tragedy, Louise became colder and more resentful. And her mouth, which had once laughed so easily at the antics of her children and smothered them with loving kisses, set into that thin, hard line.

She hated being poor and depending on the charity of her family. She hated that others had so much when she and her children had nothing of their own. Her children should have been her comfort, but she was too eaten with resentment to let their love warm her heart. Instead, she devoted herself to seeing that their lives would not be as difficult as hers. She wanted them—especially her daughters, Virginia and Isa—to acquire wealth and position. Louise would do almost anything to assure that they attain material success.

Almost anything. Louise refused to give her life to the One who would heal her heart the instant she asked Him to come inside. She rejected the Lord's saving grace and scoffed at the possibility of eternal life. To her, faith was weakness. Hadn't everything she believed in—her husband, her home, her joy—been swept away? She saw only the material world, and with every passing year, her heart grew colder and harder, like an Arctic glacier.

Don't misunderstand. Louise was not a bad person. She wouldn't rob or steal to achieve what she wanted. She had a strong sense of her duty to her children. Ever since her elderly father became ill, she'd nursed him with skill and devotion. Deep inside her, a small ember of love still glowed. But no one had been able to fan it into flame.

Aunt Louise

And so, on this brilliant June morning, she sat alone in the train and stared out the window. The splendors of God's creations were laid out before her: Rolling green hills dotted with small houses where people thanked God every day for His bounty. Flat, plowed fields in which new crops stretched upward, like hands raised in prayer, toward the sun. Orchards whose trees would soon grow heavy with fruit. Simple country churches in which people would gather at week's end to celebrate their Heavenly Father's redeeming, everlasting love.

Louise saw none of it.

After some time, she turned from the window and opened a little valise on the seat beside her. She drew out a letter and began to read it, as she'd done many times before. The letter was from her daughter Virginia, who lived in New York, and it was the last word Louise had received from Virginia in more than six months.

Louise told herself that she had no cause to worry. The letter gave no hint of problems. It was full of accounts of Virginia and her husband's busy social life—dinner with Mr. and Mrs. Rich at this fine house, calling on Mrs. Highborn at that fine house—and of Mr. Neuville's (that was Virginia's husband) most recent financial success.

Why had this been the last letter? Louise had written a number of times. Most recently, she'd written about her plans to come to New York. She had intentionally made that letter sound businesslike, with no trace of her urgent concern. She simply said that since she hadn't laid eyes on Virginia after the wedding almost three years earlier and since Vi Travilla would be staying in the city for a month, it seemed like an opportune time to make the trip.

But she'd received no reply. As she folded the letter and placed it carefully back in her valise, Louise was torn between anxiety and anger. If nothing was wrong (Louise assured herself again that nothing could be wrong), then Virginia's failure to respond was thoughtless and cruel. Virginia had always been a thoughtless girl, Louise reminded herself, and she was probably just so busy that she'd forgotten to write. Then again, Virginia had never been cruel. Of all the Conley children, Virginia had been most devoted to her mother. Then Louise had a terrible thought: *Is Virginia deliberately ignoring me? Now that she has everything I ever wanted for her, is she ashamed of her poor mother? Could she be so heartless?*

The train swayed gently back and forth as it sped along the tracks. And Louise's mind seemed to catch its rhythm. Back and forth her thoughts went. Worry, anger, worry, anger. She looked at her timepiece and saw that it was already well past noon. Another few hours and she would be in New York. But what would she find when she reached her destination?

～

Zoe, Vi, and Mrs. O'Flaherty were camped out in one of New York's most exclusive shops. Zoe—clad only in her chemise, pantaloons, and stockings—stood on a little platform in a large dressing room. Two women armed with measuring tapes bustled around her, one taking precise measurements while the other jotted the numbers in a little notebook. They repeatedly had to ask Zoe to stand still, for she tended to bounce on her toes in her excitement.

Piles of fabrics, laces, and elegant trimmings lay around the room, as well as bags and boxes containing accessories that had been purchased that day. The seamstresses would hold up a piece of cloth, wrap it about Zoe, confer on various folds and pleats and tucks in a language that sounded foreign to Vi, and then make more notes in their book.

Finishing at last, the women left. Mrs. O'Flaherty got Zoe's dress, but Zoe stood back.

"I hate to put that awful black thing on again," she said.

"Well, you will certainly cause heads to turn if you go back to the hotel in your undergarments," Mrs. O'Flaherty chuckled. She held the dress open, and Zoe stepped into it. "Stand still or I'll never get you buttoned," Mrs. O'Flaherty said. "You are as fidgety as a rabbit in a cabbage patch."

"I can't help it," Zoe said in a teasing whine. "My Papa used to say that he couldn't understand why people had to wear black when someone died. He said that we should wear bright colors because when someone goes to Heaven, that is the happiest thing there is."

"Well, very soon you will be bright as a garden at summer's height," Vi said, "though I don't understand how you can enjoy all this measuring and fitting."

"The French have a saying," Mrs. O'Flaherty said. "*Chacon son gout*. To each his own taste. Zoe enjoys shopping and getting new clothes, and Vi doesn't."

Mrs. O'Flaherty finished the last button and stood back to look at Zoe. "I have to admit that black is not your best color, Zoe."

"It's such a sad color when you have to wear it all the time," Zoe said. "Some silly rule of etiquette tells me that I must wear black for six months to show that I honor my father. But it doesn't honor him at all. He was such a happy person. He took such pleasure in every minute of life. And he made me so happy," she added with a catch in her voice.

Fearing that this conversation was, in fact, making Zoe sad, Vi asked her friend, "What did you think of our evening out with the Despards?"

"Oh, it was lovely, wasn't it?" Zoe replied, her tone lifting again. "Mrs. Despard is so beautiful, and very kind, too. And Mr. Despard was so nice to me, especially when I caused that accident. But I could see that Ed was upset. I didn't mean to embarrass him in front of his friends."

"He seemed quite all right at breakfast," Vi said.

"Do you really think so?" Zoe asked hopefully.

"I wouldn't be too concerned about Ed," Vi said as she began to gather the shopping bags they had accumulated. "He has a bit of a temper. Grandpapa says that it's a Dinsmore trait and we must all watch our tempers. But Ed gets over it quickly. You needn't worry about him."

"Oh, but I do!" Zoe exclaimed, and Vi saw the pink flush in her friend's face.

Zoe quickly went on, "I mean that I worry about you all. I want to do my best for all of you. And sometimes when I get excited, like last night, I'm not at my very best."

"Zoe Love, your coming to live with us is one of the best things that's happened in a long time," Vi said. She gave the girl a quick hug and said, "Now grab that hatbox, and we'll go. Ed is meeting Aunt Louise at the station, and we must be waiting at the hotel to greet her. If we leave Ed alone with her for too long, he will be in a temper."

~

They returned in time to freshen up and arrange for a nice tea to be sent to their suite. So all was ready when Ed and Louise arrived an hour later. Louise was courteous in her fashion and glad to see the tea and sandwiches. She hadn't eaten all day, and it was clear to everyone that she was tired. But she was not too tired to be critical. When asked about her trip, Louise complained about delays, complained about the service, complained about the dirt on the train and in the streets of New York.

Mrs. O'Flaherty kindly volunteered to help Louise unpack her things and suggested that she might prefer dinner in her room that night. Surprisingly, Louise (who rarely accepted offers of help from anyone and didn't have a high opinion of Mrs. O'Flaherty) agreed. When she'd finished her tea, she excused herself, and she and Mrs. O'Flaherty went next door to the room reserved for Louise.

"Does Aunt Louise seem a bit gloomier than usual?" Ed asked Vi as he poured himself another cup of tea.

"It's hard to tell," Vi replied. "She seemed a little more fretful than usual, but perhaps it's just fatigue. I'm sure she's looking forward to seeing Virginia."

"Well, that's odd too," Ed said. "I asked her about Virginia on the ride back to the hotel, and she hardly said anything. None of the usual bragging about Virginia's well-to-do husband and fancy townhouse. Last night, I asked Chris Despard if he knew Henry Neuville, and Chris has never heard of him. That's strange because Chris knows just about everybody in the financial trade."

"Umm," Vi said. "No one can know everybody in a city as big as this. Perhaps Mr. Neuville is in a different type of business than Mr. Despard."

"Have you never met your cousin's husband?" Zoe asked.

Vi thought for a moment. "Now that you ask, I realize that none of the family has met him, except Aunt Louise, of course."

Violet's Turning Point

Vi explained that Virginia had married three summers ago, when the rest of the family was at Viamede, their Louisiana estate. At the invitation of Louise's wealthy sister-in-law, Louise and Virginia had gone to a vacation spot in the Hudson Valley. Mr. Neuville was a guest at their hotel. He had courted Virginia, and they became engaged. The wedding took place before anyone knew anything about it, and the newly married Mr. and Mrs. Neuville moved to New York City. The family was not informed until Louise returned to Roselands.

"From the way Aunt Louise talked back then, you'd have thought Virginia married the Prince of Wales," Ed said with a laugh. "I never wondered before why Virginia hasn't come back for a visit at Roselands. I just assumed that she was enjoying not being under Aunt Louise's thumb for the first time in her life."

"But she didn't even come to Isa's wedding," Vi said. Turning to Zoe, Vi went on, "Cousin Isa is Virginia's sister, and one of the nicest people you could ever know. She's married to James Keith, who's our cousin but not hers, and they live at Viamede. James is chaplain there and also the pastor at a local church. You'll get to meet them the next time we visit Louisiana."

Zoe giggled and said, "I will need a chart to understand your large family. Cousins and not cousins? It is very complicated."

"We all have trouble keeping everyone straight," Ed agreed. "The question now is where Mr. Neuville fits in. I wonder who he is."

Vi took a last sandwich and said, "We should know more tomorrow. Oh, I wish you could stay an extra day or two, Ed. Do you really have to leave in the morning?"

segmentTag# Aunt Louise

"I'd like to stay, but my seminar starts next Monday, and I have some studying to do beforehand. Besides, you girls are too busy with your shopping and social engagements to miss me. You're visiting Marguerite Despard on Friday, aren't you?"

Zoe nodded her head and said, "She is such an interesting person, Ed. Thank you very much for introducing me to her. She said that there will be several people there who are 'in the arts.' What does she mean by that? Will they be artists?"

"More likely some people who are interested in the museum. Maybe some art dealers," Ed said. "Mr. and Mrs. Despard are collectors, and she is a great fan of the modern art from France. Frankly, I don't know what she sees in the stuff."

"Art is not 'stuff'," Zoe said a little sharply. But she caught herself and smiled at Ed, saying, "I just mean that different people have different tastes."

Vi stood and addressed her brother, "Well then, tonight will be your going-away, Ed. Where do you propose we eat?"

Ed suggested a restaurant near the hotel. Then he excused himself, for he wanted to pack his bag and do a little reading before dinner. "Be sure that Mrs. O'Flaherty can dine with us," he said as he was leaving. "Since Aunt Louise will have supper in her room, the four of us will make a jolly party."

It was indeed a merry evening, and they all returned to the hotel in high spirits. But Ed begged off further conversation, for his train departed very early the next morning. Since he would not see Vi before he left, he asked his sister to accompany him to his room.

When they were alone, he said, "If there's anything you need, you can telegraph me."

"I think we'll be fine," Vi said with a little smile. "Mrs. O'Flaherty will keep us on the straight and narrow."

"If it were just you and Mrs. O, I wouldn't worry, but I can't shake this feeling that something odd is going on with Aunt Louise and Virginia. And there's young Zoe. She can be a handful, Vi, so keep your guard up. I really wonder that Mamma made you responsible for her."

"I thought we settled this last night," Vi replied with a frown.

"We did," Ed said, patting her arm. "Zoe's a good kid, I guess. But she's impetuous, Vi. It's pretty obvious that her father spoiled her, and she hasn't learned to think about the consequences of her actions. I'm always wondering what she'll do next."

"I don't think she's spoiled at all," Vi said firmly. "I know her much better than you do, Ed, and I know how trustworthy she is. Maybe you need to ask yourself where this prejudice against her comes from."

Ed stepped back, and Vi saw a look of hurt in his face. "It's not prejudice," he protested. "I'm just concerned for you. And for Zoe, too."

"Well, stop worrying yourself," Vi said with a confident smile. "Zoe is my responsibility, and I think I'm up to the task of watching out for her. My goodness, sometimes you act just like Grandpapa. I imagine that you've been pacing the floor thinking about all the trouble Zoe and I could get into. Just keep us in your prayers, big brother, and everything will be all right. We'll see Virginia, and Zoe will get her new clothes and we'll go to the museums and historic sites. But it won't be much fun if I know you're at school pacing the floors and wringing your hands."

He laughed, "I admit to the pacing, but I never wring my hands. Okay then, little sister, I agree not to worry so long as you promise to write me about all you are doing."

Vi hugged him. "I'll miss you, Ed," she said. "These last few days have been such fun."

"And I'll miss you," he replied. Then he held her at arm's length and his eyes twinkled as he added, "But I think I've been in the henhouse for too long. It will be good to get back to my books and away from all the talk of bustles and flounces and such stuff as you ladies have subjected me to."

"Oh, you poor thing," Vi teased. "Well, kiss me good-bye, and I will return to the henhouse."

He did as he was told, kissing her cheek. Then he said, "I really will miss you, Vi. You're so grown up now, and just the best company. I guess you can handle Zoe and Aunt Louise. But as I said, if you need me, I can be here in just a few hours."

When she had settled into bed, Vi opened her Bible and turned to the first chapter of James. The verse she sought was the last: "Religion that God our Father accepts as pure and faultless is this: to look after orphans and widows in their distress and to keep oneself from being polluted by the world."

She considered her responsibilities. She was grown up now, and that meant taking responsibility for others. Widows and orphans. Her Aunt Louise and her friend Zoe.

Violet's Turning Point

Then she prayed, "Please, Lord, help me be a vigilant guardian for Zoe. And help me to help my Aunt Louise if I can. I know how hard my aunt's life has been. I want to reach out to her with love and understanding. It's easy to love people who are lovable, but my challenge is to love those who are not easy. Please help me to be responsible and guide me to do what's right for everyone. And thank You, Lord, for being at my side whatever happens."

After asking for His blessing on Ed and Mrs. O'Flaherty and all her family, Vi ended her prayer, put her Bible on the bedside table, and turned out the lamp. But just before she fell asleep, a question darted across her mind almost like a flying bird that one sees for an instant from the corner of one's eye. *Where is Virginia?* It flickered, and then it was gone.

CHAPTER

A Disappointing Search

*For I am afraid that when I come
I may not find you as I want
you to be, and you may not
find me as you want
me to be.*

2 CORINTHIANS 12:20

A Disappointing Search

$\mathcal{E}$d had left the hotel an hour before Vi awoke, and his train was far from the great city when Vi joined Zoe and Mrs. O'Flaherty for breakfast in the hotel dining room.

"Is Aunt Louise coming?" she asked as a waiter held her chair and she sat down. "Should we wait for her before we order?"

"No need," Zoe whispered. She nodded her head slightly toward the entrance to the dining room, and Vi turned. Her aunt was walking briskly toward their table — head high and eyes forward as if there were no one else in the room.

A young waiter quickly appeared and held Louise's chair. She sat down but didn't trouble herself to say thanks.

"You look rested, Aunt Louise," Vi said pleasantly.

"That's surprising considering all the noise in the streets," Louise replied. "The carts and horses were clattering before dawn. I couldn't get back to sleep. And the mattress was as hard as a board."

"You'll get used to the city noise, Mrs. Conley," said Zoe helpfully. "It's always hard at first when you're used to the quiet of the country. For me it was the opposite. When I first came from Rome to live at The Oaks, it was the silence that kept me awake."

Louise looked down her nose at the girl and said, "You speak as if I were some country clod who had never been to the city before. I assure you, Miss Love, that I don't need anyone's advice about city life." Then Louise picked up her menu and began to read.

Vi looked at Zoe and saw tears in her friend's eyes. Vi was furious. Her cheeks were hot with anger. She made

49

herself count slowly to ten before she said, "Zoe did not intend to advise you, Aunt Louise. She was being sympathetic."

"Perhaps," Louise replied coldly. Then she laid her menu aside and said, "I shall have a three-minute egg, buttered toast, marmalade, and tea with milk."

Understandably, Vi, Zoe, and Mrs. O'Flaherty hurried through their breakfasts. Louise was still eating when they all rose to excuse themselves.

Vi addressed her aunt rather stiffly. She said, "I'm sorry to leave, but we have an appointment with the dressmaker."

Louise looked up, and Vi saw something strange in her aunt's eyes. If it had been anyone else, Vi would have thought it a look of panic. But it vanished quickly, and Louise said, "Will you stay a moment, Violet? I have something I need to say in private. Your companions may go on."

Luckily, Louise didn't see the wink that Mrs. O'Flaherty gave to Zoe or Zoe's impish smile.

"We'll be waiting in the suite," Mrs. O'Flaherty told Vi, and she and Zoe walked away.

"What is it, Aunt Louise?" Vi asked, trying to keep her voice even.

Placing her teacup on its saucer, Louise said, "I would like you to join me today. I will be going to Virginia's house, and I am not sure of my way about the city."

"The hotel will get you a driver who knows the way," Vi replied.

"I understand that, Vi, but I do not think it proper for a lady to go about on her own in the city," Louise said briskly. Then looking down at the table as if she were inspecting it for crumbs, Louise added in a strangely soft tone, "I would be very grateful if you could accompany me."

A Disappointing Search

There was something about the request—so unlike Louise—that made Vi answer without any thought. "I'll be glad to go with you," she said.

"Then hurry up to the suite and tell the others," Louise said, her voice back to its usual chilly, commanding tone. "I shall arrange for a carriage and meet you in the lobby in twenty minutes."

"Do you have Virginia's address?" Vi asked.

"Of course I do," Louise replied.

Vi couldn't see how tightly Louise was clutching the purse in her lap. Nor could she see the worn envelope inside it.

Precisely twenty minutes later, Vi and Louise were helped into an open carriage by the hotel doorman. Louise gave the driver an address in the Gramercy Park area, and they were off.

Vi tried to make pleasant conversation with her aunt. She asked about Virginia and Mr. Neuville, but received only the most curt of replies. Vi commented on the beauty of the park, the impressive city buildings and houses they passed as the carriage moved southward on Fifth Avenue, the fashionable women and men who strolled the sidewalks, the fine weather. But Louise responded with little more than grunts and heavy sighs. So Vi finally gave up her efforts to be polite and decided to enjoy the passing scene in silence.

Eventually the carriage turned left off the main thoroughfare and onto cobblestone residential streets. There were some individual homes with large lawns and gardens, but most of the houses were built in rows of three- and four-story buildings attached to one another. Some had shallow front gardens, but most were entered directly from the sidewalks. There was a great deal of activity. Servants swept steps and sidewalks; workers carried boxes of fresh vegetables and fruits to the houses from their carts and wagons; nursemaids pushing baby carriages stopped to chat under the shade trees that marched in a line down the sidewalks. It was a typical summer morning on the streets where New York's well-to-do made their homes.

The carriage came to a stop before a handsome house in an elegant row, and the driver informed them that this was the address they sought. He helped them down, and Vi handed him the money for their fare. Then she gave him extra coins and asked him to remain until they were inside.

Vi and Louise stood for some moments and looked up at the house. It was larger than the other houses on the street. It was separated from the sidewalk by an iron fence and gate. Its small front garden bloomed with fragrant roses, and a brick walkway led to wide stone steps edged with elaborate iron handrails. The house was built of a dark brown stone that made Vi think of chocolate, but its tall windows were trimmed in white and the sunlight glinted off the glass. It was an imposing façade, Vi thought, but a welcoming one.

Louise folded up her parasol, and they proceeded through the gate, along the short path, and up the steps to the front door. Louise rang the bell, and after just a few moments, the door was opened. A middle-aged man in a butler's dark suit greeted them.

"May I help you?" he asked courteously.

"We would like to see Mrs. Neuville," Louise said.

A Disappointing Search

Nothing registered in the butler's face as he said, "Whom did you wish to see, madam?"

"Mrs. Neuville," Louise replied with impatience. "Mrs. Henry Neuville."

"I am afraid there is no one here by that name," the man said. "Perhaps you have the wrong address."

"This is *not* the wrong address," Louise said forcefully. "Mrs. Neuville is my daughter, and this is her home."

The butler's voice did not change as he said, "I am very sorry, but this is the home of Mr. and Mrs. Vangelt."

"But it can't be!" Louise exclaimed.

"I have worked for the Vangelts for ten years, ma'am, and I can assure you that this has always been their home," the butler said. His voice remained as calm and polite as when he greeted them. But Vi saw a flash of worry cross his face.

Louise began fumbling in her purse, so Vi asked the butler if perhaps the Neuvilles might live in one of the neighboring houses. He was explaining that he had never heard of Mr. and Mrs. Neuville when Louise reached out and waved an envelope in his face.

"This is a letter from my daughter," she said, her tone shaky. "Look. You can see the return address."

The butler took the envelope and read it. "Yes," he said calmly, "this is the address, but I can assure you, madam, that this is the Vangelt residence. No one by the name of Neuville lives here or works here."

Louise exploded, "Works! Of course my daughter does not work here." Then she turned sharply on her heel and rushed back to the street.

The butler looked questioningly at Vi.

"I apologize for my aunt," Vi said. "She has traveled a long way, and this is a disappointment for her."

The butler smiled and handed the envelope to Vi. "I understand," he said. "It is clearly a mistake. I'm sure she will find her daughter."

"Yes," Vi said a little uneasily. "I'm sure she will. Thank you."

She started to leave but turned back before the butler could close the door.

"Is Mrs. Vangelt at home by any chance?" she asked.

"No, ma'am," he said. "She is away for the day."

"Then would you give her this?" Vi said. She took her calling card case from her purse and removed a crisp, white card and a small pencil. Quickly, she wrote the name of her hotel below her engraved name. On the back, she wrote: "Do you know of Mrs. Henry Neuville? Mrs. Virginia Conley Neuville?" She handed the card to the man and said, "It is possible that Mrs. Neuville may have visited here at one time. Your employer might recognize the name."

"Perhaps she may," the butler said kindly. He looked closely at the card and added, "I will see that Mrs. Vangelt gets your card, Miss Travilla."

Vi thanked him again and left. The man gazed at her until both Vi and her aunt were again in the carriage. With a feeling of both concern and pity, he slowly shut the door. Then he placed Vi's card in a small silver bowl on a side table in the foyer and went back to his duties.

Vi directed the carriage driver to return to the hotel and took her seat beside Louise. She could see that her aunt was very pale and that her hands were trembling.

But Louise's voice was like solid ice when she said, "That stupid man. That very stupid man."

"We'll find Virginia," Vi said. "There's obviously been an error. Virginia might have been staying at this house when

she wrote the letter. She might have been a guest of the Vangelts. That would explain the address."

"Yes, that's probably just what happened," Louise said as much to herself as to Vi. "That man was too stupid to remember her name. It will be easy enough to straighten out the mistake. Virginia probably lives quite near. We could be passing her house this very moment."

Vi said, "It will be all right, Aunt Louise. We'll find her."

She hoped her voice was reassuring, and Louise did settle back a little more comfortably against her seat. Nothing else was said on the ride back to the hotel, but Vi was thinking a great many thoughts. In her bewilderment, she wondered just how they could "straighten out the mistake." *How does one go about finding a lost person in a city like New York?* she asked herself. Feeling completely at a loss to know how to proceed, she prayed, *Lord, please help us find Virginia. Help me to know what to do.*

"You could hire a detective," Zoe suggested. "I've read about them in stories. They solve ever so many kinds of mysteries."

"I don't think we need to do that yet," said Mrs. O'Flaherty.

Vi, Zoe, and Mrs. O'Flaherty were in the sitting room of their suite after their dinner. Louise had gone directly to her own room when she and Vi returned to the hotel. She hadn't wanted to discuss the problem further. Insisting that she had no appetite, she said she would nap and then have an early supper in her room. She made it clear that she didn't want to see anyone that night.

Violet's Turning Point

When Zoe and Mrs. O'Flaherty got back from their shopping, Vi told them what had happened and they began to discuss what they could do.

"Should we inform the police?" Vi asked.

"I think we should try other avenues first," Mrs. O'Flaherty replied. "Now, girls, we must be logical. We must ask ourselves who might know where Mr. and Mrs. Neuville are. Are you acquainted with any of their friends?"

"No," Vi sighed. But the question jogged her memory. *The butler gave me the envelope with Virginia's return address,* she thought, *and it's still in my purse. There might be something in the letter — Virginia might have written about a friend who would know her address. But would it be right to read her letter?* She had never before in her life considered reading another person's private correspondence.

"I have Virginia's letter to Aunt Louise," she said slowly.

"Then read it!" Zoe exclaimed. "There might be a clue in it."

Vi turned to Mrs. O'Flaherty and asked, "Should we?"

Mrs. O'Flaherty's expression was very thoughtful. "Not in normal circumstances," she said. "Even in this case, I'm not inclined to read another person's letter. It may be necessary if we cannot think of a better idea. Still, I believe it should be Mrs. Conley's decision to tell us what her daughter wrote. You can ask her tomorrow, Vi girl."

Zoe slumped against a pillow with a disappointed sigh. She wasn't interested in what Virginia might have written to her mother. But she was very curious about the mystery of Virginia's whereabouts. In the stories she read, detectives were always finding important clues in letters.

"What does Mr. Neuville do?" Mrs. O'Flaherty was asking Vi.

"He's in some kind of financial business," Vi said. "I don't know what it is."

"Then perhaps we have a place to begin," Mrs. O'Flaherty said in an encouraging tone. "You know your mother's lawyer and business agents here in New York."

Vi said excitedly, "Of course! We can ask them for help. We can see Mr. Phillips tomorrow. He's Mamma's lawyer here. Surely he can tell us what is best to do."

"Don't forget the Despards," Zoe said. "Mr. Despard is a banker or something like that. He might help. And we're going there for tea tomorrow."

Vi remembered what Ed had told her. "Mr. Despard doesn't know Mr. Neuville," Vi said. "Ed asked him when we were at dinner."

Zoe could not be dissuaded. "But he might know someone who does know. That's what happens in detective stories. You have to keep asking lots of questions of everybody until you get the answers you need. Then you have to fit the answers together like a puzzle."

Mrs. O'Flaherty said with a gentle smile, "This isn't a detective story, Zoe, but it is a puzzle. We can solve it if we use the minds God has blessed us with and ask Him to help us. Just keep in mind that this puzzle involves real people with real feelings. We must never forget that Mrs. Conley loves her daughter. However she may pretend not to need our help, she deserves our understanding and support."

"Let's pray," Vi said suddenly. "The book of James says, 'Is any one of you in trouble? He should pray. Is anyone happy? Let him sing songs of praise.' Let's ask our Heavenly Father to deliver us from this trouble and guide us to Virginia."

Violet's Turning Point

They held hands and bowed their heads. Vi began the prayer; then Mrs. O'Flaherty and Zoe added their thanks to God for hearing their entreaties. When they finished, each of them went to their beds with lighter hearts, full of hope and renewed determination.

CHAPTER

5

Another Journey

He reveals the deep things of
darkness and brings deep
shadows into the
light.

JOB 12:22

Another Journey

*A*fter she had dressed and said her prayers the next morning, Vi wrote to Mr. Phillips. If the lawyer could see her that day, then their search for Virginia might begin in earnest.

Breakfast was waiting in the sitting room when Vi entered. Louise and Zoe were already at the little dining table, and Vi noticed that her aunt looked very tired and her eyes were rimmed in red. Zoe was unusually quiet.

"Did you oversleep, Violet?" Louise asked in a sharp tone.

"No, Aunt," Vi said sweetly as she sat down, "I had an important letter to write."

They all began to eat, and after several minutes, Vi inquired where Mrs. O'Flaherty was.

"She went to the lobby to buy a newspaper," Zoe said. "We must be sure to save some ham and eggs for her. She'll be hungry when she gets back."

Suddenly, Louise slammed her hand on the table, banging her fork against her plate.

"I simply do not understand why I am expected to dine with a servant!" she burst out. "An Irish shanty woman like your Mrs. O'Flaherty should know her place! She should know not to expect equal treatment from her betters!"

Vi looked at her aunt in astonishment. Louise's face was almost purple with rage. Her mouth was hard and thin, and tears trembled in her eyes.

Without thinking, Zoe protested, "Mrs. O'Flaherty is not—"

Louise cut her off by jumping up from her chair and exclaiming, "I don't care what she is or isn't! I don't care about anything except—except . . ."

Then she ran from the room, and a second later they heard a door slam.

"I didn't mean to . . ." Zoe began.

"You didn't do anything wrong," Vi said. "Aunt Louise must be terribly upset about Virginia, but she never shows her feelings. She holds them inside, and what she does show is misplaced anger toward others. She's been that way as long as I can remember. We have to be patient with her."

"Is that what Mrs. O meant about your aunt needing our understanding?" Zoe asked.

"Yes," Vi sighed, "though it seems nearly impossible sometimes. She's a difficult person to understand. I certainly don't understand her. But I'll talk to her, after she's had some time to calm down. We should finish our breakfast. I wonder what's keeping Mrs. O?"

As if in answer to Vi's question, Mrs. O'Flaherty came in the door at just that moment. It was comforting to both girls to see her tall, strong figure and smiling face. She sat down and poured herself a cup of coffee while Vi told her what had just occurred.

Mrs. O'Flaherty laughed heartily when told that she'd been called an "Irish shanty woman."

"Is that a bad thing?" Zoe asked. She couldn't imagine anyone saying cruel words about Mrs. O'Flaherty.

"Mrs. Conley probably thinks it's bad," Mrs. O'Flaherty replied. "A shanty is just a poor house, like a hut or a shack. But Mrs. Conley wasn't really angry about sharing her table with a poor working woman from Ireland. She's in a great deal of pain, not knowing where her daughter is. She happened to take out her pain and worry on me. She uses her coldness to shield herself from pain. The trouble is that a cold heart is a poor shield. Ice always cracks under pressure."

"Oh, I wish she'd let God warm her heart," Zoe said with a pout. "Then she would stop being so unhappy and hateful to other people."

"Well, God works in mysterious ways," Mrs. O'Flaherty said gently. "This is a very hard time for her, but maybe her heart's melting even now."

"It would be nice to see Aunt Louise happy," Vi said. She laid her napkin on the table. "I guess I should go to her now."

"Would you like me to speak with her?" Mrs. O'Flaherty asked.

Vi almost said "yes," but she knew that Louise was her responsibility. *Orphans and widows*, she reminded herself.

"I'll do it," she said. "I can tell her that I've written to Mr. Phillips and that he will surely help us find Virginia." She laid her neat white envelope on the table and added, "Before I talk to Aunt Louise, I'll take my letter downstairs to the hotel manager so it can be delivered as soon as possible."

They finished their breakfast, and Zoe and Mrs. O'Flaherty went to their rooms. Vi was putting on her jacket to go to the hotel lobby when there was a tapping at the door. "Come in," she said, thinking it was someone from the kitchen staff who'd come to collect the breakfast trays. But when the door opened, she saw the hotel manager himself.

He held out an envelope almost exactly like her own. "This was just delivered for you, Miss Travilla," the manager said in an affable way. "I thought it might be important. I can wait if you would like to send a reply."

The manager would not normally deliver letters to hotel guests. But he had recognized the name on the return address. "Vangelt" was an important name in the city.

Vi took the envelope and asked him to be seated. She opened it quickly and read:

Violet's Turning Point

Dear Miss Travilla,

My butler informed me that you called, and I regret that I was not at home. I know your lovely mother, and I should like to meet her daughter.

I understand from my butler and your note that you were hoping to find a "Mrs. Virginia Conley Neuville" at my house. I do not know anyone named Neuville. But as I thought about it, I remembered a Miss Virginia Newman who worked as my personal secretary until about six months ago. She was a charming young woman and very efficient. I was sad to lose her. Just before Christmas, she had to return to the South to care for her mother, who was ill. It was a sudden departure, and I have not heard from Miss Newman since. However, she left a New York address to which I sent her final payment. This is probably not the person you seek, but I am enclosing the address in case it may be helpful to you.

The letter went on to invite Vi to tea at a convenient time, and it was signed "Mrs. Maurice Vangelt." Inside the envelope, Vi found a small card.

The hotel manager had been regarding Vi with intense curiosity, but his face took on a bland expression as she looked up from the letter.

"Do you mind waiting just a few minutes?" she asked. "I will write a reply very quickly."

"Delighted to," the manager said with a practiced smile. He was an ambitious man, and he believed that providing personal service for wealthy guests was always good business. He wouldn't miss this chance to be helpful to a Travilla *and* a Vangelt.

Another Journey

Vi hurried to her room and wrote a gracious note, accepting Mrs. Vangelt's invitation to tea and thanking her for the information. Then she returned to the sitting room and gave the note to the manager. She considered giving him her letter to Mr. Phillips as well. But she thought that it might not be necessary now—if Mrs. Vangelt's information proved useful.

The manager promised to send Vi's thank-you note immediately. He bowed, and still smiling, left to complete his task.

Vi read the letter again and looked at the address on the card. *I've never heard of this street, but that doesn't mean anything,* Vi thought. She was familiar with the city, but she hardly knew every neighborhood.

It was time to talk with her aunt. With a little prayer for patience, Vi squared her shoulders, and with Mrs. Vangelt's letter in hand, she went to Louise's room.

An hour later, Vi and Louise were standing in front of the hotel, waiting for the doorman to hail a carriage for them.

Louise was nervous and fretful. As always, she complained about everything. The doorman was too slow, she said. The day was too overcast. The street was too crowded. And their venture in the city was pointless.

"Would you rather not go?" Vi asked.

"Of course we must go," Louise replied as if Vi's question were ridiculous. "I am just saying that this person—this Virginia Newman—cannot be my Virginia. But we must check as a courtesy to Mrs. Vangelt. She is one of the most important people in New York society."

Louise's thinking made no sense to Vi, but she understood that her aunt was creating excuses for herself.

Violet's Turning Point

"It's impossible that Virginia would have worked as anyone's secretary," Louise went on in her haughtiest way. "But it would be rude to ignore Mrs. Vangelt's note. That is the only reason for this fool's errand, but it is reason enough. Mrs. Vangelt is not someone whom we should offend."

An open carriage pulled up to the curb, and the hotel doorman helped the ladies in. The driver looked back over his shoulder and asked where they would like to go.

When Vi gave him the address, he looked at her strangely. Thinking he hadn't understood her, Vi repeated the address.

The driver replied only, "As you say, ma'am." But Vi saw the way he shrugged his shoulders and shook his head as he faced forward and reined the horse into the street.

At her side, Louise was complaining about something, but Vi didn't hear her aunt. She was beginning to worry about where they were going and what they would find when they got there.

~⟶

At first the carriage seemed to be traveling the same route they had followed to Mrs. Vangelt's. But after two blocks, it turned off the fashionable street. It wasn't long before Vi realized that they were in neighborhoods she'd never seen. Elegant houses had given way to simpler rows of dwellings. There were more open-air shops and sellers' carts and more people out shopping. The feeling was homely and comfortable.

Gradually the scene changed again. The streets were narrower and became rutted and broken, but in spite of their poor condition, the carriage driver cracked his whip in the air, speeding the horse's pace. Instead of neat, middle-class homes and shops, everything looked old and dirty and bedraggled. Some of the streets they passed were no more than dried mud paths lined with crumbling tenements and huts. Poorly dressed men with sorrowful eyes sat in doorways and lounged on street corners. They stared at the carriage as it passed, and some laughed in an unpleasant way. Children in ragged clothing played in the streets with no one to watch over them. The air smelled stagnant and foul.

Louise said several times that they must be going the wrong way. She declared that they should be heading west, not east toward the river. But somehow Vi knew that they were on the right track. She was remembering what Dr. Frazier had said about the city—that it was like an onion and that the poor lived in the outer rings.

Louise was threatening to stop the carriage and have the driver return to the hotel when the vehicle turned into a street of somewhat better-kept buildings. It was not a wealthy or middleclass neighborhood by any means, but different from the ones they had just passed through. There were scraggly trees here and there, and the people walking on the sidewalks seemed to have more purpose. The carriage slowly turned a corner and Vi heard some women talking as they shopped at a cart piled with old clothes and household items. She picked up words in foreign languages and heavily accented English. She was reminded of the street where the Constanza family dwelt in Rome—where she and Zoe had taken little Alberto home to his widowed mother and sister. Her mind flashed back to that day, and she saw again the impoverished rooms in which the Constanza family lived. She tried to imagine her cousin Virginia in rooms such as those, but it wasn't possible. *Surely Aunt Louise is right and this is a fool's errand*, Vi thought. *I should tell the driver to take us back to the hotel.* But something told her not to doubt, and she reminded herself to trust the path the Lord had set. Whatever the destination, He would lead her aright.

A few moments later, the carriage halted before a row house that was clearly more run-down than most. Its paint had mostly peeled away, and a number of its windows were cracked and covered with yellowed newspaper. On its upper floor, a broken shutter hung beside a boarded-over window and looked as if it might fall to the ground at any minute. The open space that led down to the basement level was filled with trash, empty bottles, and broken bits of furniture.

Vi paid the driver. As she'd done the previous day, she gave him extra coins and asked him to wait. But this driver was not so accommodating. He agreed to stay only after Vi offered him a handsome payment to remain and then take them back to the hotel. When he asked how long the ladies would be, Vi told him perhaps only a few minutes, but certainly no more than an hour. He didn't seem happy, but the promise of a large fee overcame whatever it was that worried him.

Vi and Louise climbed the unswept steps to the doorway. Vi spotted a rusted letter box with a large nameplate above it. The nameplate contained many slots where tenants would put their name cards. Most of the slots were empty, but a few held dirty, weathered cards with scrawled names. One of the cards read "Neuville 2-B."

"That means nothing," Louise said as she opened the door into a dark, musty entry hall. "There must be many people named Neuville." But she did not turn back.

There were stairs directly in front of them, and as they began to climb, Louise continued complaining about their "wild goose chase."

Another Journey

Vi had to fight back her own doubts again. She couldn't imagine Virginia living in a place like this. The stairs were filthy and littered with paper, pieces of broken glass, and frayed bits of what might once have been carpet. The steps were worn to splinters in some places, and they groaned ominously with every step.

They reached the first landing and looked at the four closed doors along the narrow hallway. Each door had a faded painted number. They found 2-B, but instead of knocking, Louise stared around at the grimy and torn wallpaper and cracked plaster, the trash on the floors—old cans and bottles, pieces of torn cloth and broken wood, and thick dust and dirt that someone had tried to sweep into a pile. An old broom stood in a corner, its head upward; its bristles were broken and caked with dirt. It looked to Vi like a scarecrow that had been picked clean of its ornaments.

The one window in the hall was cracked; its lower half had been nailed over with pieces of wood, and torn, stained curtains kept out most of the light. There was no glow of gaslight as in the hotel, and with so little light, the walls seemed to close in. Vi remembered an incident from her childhood, when she'd accidentally locked herself in her brother's closet and screamed in panic before Ed rescued her.

They heard muffled voices from the floor above, but this level was oddly quiet, and there seemed to be barely enough air to breathe. The hall was much hotter than outside, and it smelled of stale food and mustiness.

There was a rustling near the broom in the corner, and from the corner of her eye, Vi thought she saw a quick movement. A mouse? Or something worse?

Vi suddenly did not want to remain in this grim place a moment longer than necessary. So she knocked impatiently at the door of 2-B. There was no response. Then Louise knocked. Still nothing. She knocked harder until she was pounding the door with her fist.

She was about to give up when they heard something—a metallic rattle like a chain—and the door opened. Standing before them was a terribly thin young woman whose face was as pale as a sheet. There were dark circles below her eyes and two flaming red circles on her ghostly cheeks. She wore a tattered dressing gown that had once been beautiful, and her tangled hair hung limply over her shoulders.

She looked at them almost as if they weren't there. But then she focused her attention on Louise, and in a strangled whisper, she said, "Mother? Is that you?"

Virginia almost fell into Louise's arms. Despite her shock, Louise grasped her daughter and held her up.

"What has happened to you?" Louise finally managed to say.

Vi immediately realized that Virginia was too overcome to speak. She told Louise to take one of Virginia's arms, and she took the other. Vi could feel how fragile her cousin was.

Virginia managed to help a little as they carried her into the apartment and settled her on a torn sofa. "You're ill," Louise was saying. "Where is your husband? Where is Mr. Neuville? Did he leave you like this? Why would he leave you? How did you get to this place?"

Louise's voice and her questions sounded harsh. But all the while, she was holding Virginia close to her and rocking her as if she were a small child. She stroked Virginia's hair and forehead.

"You have a fever," Louise said in a choked voice. She looked up at Vi, and her gray eyes were dark with fear.

Vi quickly surveyed the room. Except for the sofa and a small table, it was bare of furniture. Curtains hung over the windows, but they were so tattered that light entered the room and exposed its utter shabbiness. There was a door at the far side of the room and beside it a little nook that might be a kitchen. Swiftly, Vi went to the nook, which was no bigger than a closet, and found a pitcher of water and a cloth that seemed clean. She poured some water into a chipped bowl and soaked the cloth. She took it to Louise, who began gently wiping Virginia's brow.

Vi had seen a little burner in the kitchen and hoped to make some tea for Virginia. But there was nothing on the shelves. No tea or sugar or food of any kind. Only an empty bottle that had contained milk.

How much at that moment Vi wished that Mrs. O'Flaherty or her mother were there. They would know what to do. *Dear Lord, help me think*, Vi prayed. *Tell me what I must do.*

Then she remembered that the driver was waiting outside.

"Aunt Louise, we must take Virginia to a doctor," she said. "I'll get the carriage driver to help. I'll be right back."

She rushed from the room into the stifling hallway. She ran down the stairs and out of the house. Breathlessly, she told the driver that there was an ill woman inside and that he must carry her down the stairs to the carriage.

"What's the matter with her?" the driver asked. He knew all too well about the diseases that could rampage through these poor neighborhoods, killing hundreds in their wake.

"I think it's pneumonia," Vi said. "Not contagious. She has to get to a doctor."

"The hospital's a long way off, and there's no doctor around here," the driver said.

"Yes, there is!" Vi almost cried. Her little purse was hanging over her arm, and she drew out her card case. Inside was a business card she had stuck there on the night they dined with the Despards at Domenici's.

Violet's Turning Point

She showed it to the driver. "See? Dr. Amelia Frazier! And that's her address. It's a clinic, and it must be close."

The driver studied the card and said, "It's closer than the hospital. All right, I'll help if you're sure it's not something catching. I can't be taking any kind of sickness home to my wife and children."

"I'm almost sure, I promise," Vi said. "Follow me upstairs."

The driver was a strong man, and he easily lifted Virginia from the sofa. Louise had wrapped her in a blanket, and she followed the man as they left the apartment. Virginia seemed delirious; she kept saying some word over and over. Vi thought it was "bed" or "bedside."

It would only take a few seconds to check. Vi ran back into the apartment and opened the door she had seen. The room was dark and cluttered, though she could make out a bed. There was a box of some sort on the bed. *Maybe that's what Virginia wants*, Vi thought.

She moved toward the bed, banging her shin against something. She saw that the thing on the bed was an open travel case—a small one. For an instant, she felt annoyed that Virginia apparently wanted clothes. But then she heard a sound. It was as soft as a kitten's whimper. Vi looked into the case and saw a bundle of something like towels. The sound came again and the bundle moved. Peering closely, Vi saw a tiny hand appear.

Ever so gently, she pulled back some of the cloth. Two small eyes glistened at her. Carefully, Vi lifted the bundle and cradled the baby in her arms. She placed her fingers on its forehead and felt the burning heat of fever.

6

A Cautious Diagnosis

For he has rescued us from the dominion of darkness and brought us into the kingdom of the Son he loves.

COLOSSIANS 1:13

A Cautious Diagnosis

Vi had forgotten all about having tea at the Despards'. But when they reached Dr. Frazier's clinic, she remembered to write a quick note to Mrs. O'Flaherty, explaining what had happened and where they were. She assured Mrs. O'Flaherty that she and Louise were fine and would return when they could.

The carriage driver had stayed at the clinic. He felt out of place among the mothers and small children who crowded the waiting room. But he had a good heart, and he could not bring himself to leave until he knew that the ill woman and the infant were safe. It was about a half hour before Vi came to him. She told him that Virginia was indeed very ill with fever, but the doctor said it was not a contagious disease.

"And the baby?" the driver asked.

Vi lowered her eyes and said, "The doctor is with the baby now. I don't know anything yet."

The driver said, "Poor wee thing. I have little ones of my own. I know the helpless feeling when one of them is sick."

"What is your name?" Vi asked.

"Meriweather, ma'am," he said. "Kevin Meriweather."

"Mr. Meriweather," she said, "I don't know what we would have done without you. I was wondering if you would do one more thing. I have a letter for my companions at the hotel. Could you take it?"

"That's no problem, ma'am," he said. "I'll do it quick enough."

Vi opened her little purse and said, "I'm afraid I don't have enough money with me to pay for all your time, but . . ."

Mr. Meriweather put up his hand and said, "We can set-tle up later. I'm always picking up folks at your hotel. I can see you sometime—when the lady and the baby are well."

"That's very thoughtful of you," Vi said with a lovely smile. "I insist that you take this"—she held out some bills—"as a down payment."

He took the money and said, "You're going to need transportation later on. What's say I come back here about four o'clock? I can wait for you until you're ready to leave."

"But it may be a long wait, and your family will be expecting you."

"That's no problem, ma'am. My wife, God bless her, is used to my long hours, and she'd have my head if I didn't do what I could for that poor mother and baby. Just give me that letter, and I'll be on my way."

Vi watched him leave. *There is so much goodness in the world*, she thought. *Thank You, dear Lord, for people like Mr. Meriweather, and for reminding me that the light of Your loving Spirit shines all around us. It shines in unexpected places.*

A hand touched her arm, and she turned to see Dr. Frazier standing beside her.

"It's good that you got your cousin to us so quickly," the doctor said. "Another day and pneumonia would surely have set in. She's very weak but not so ill as I first thought. I was fearful I might find tuberculosis, but her lungs are clear, and her fever is already subsiding. Assuming that all goes well, she will need lots of care to recuperate. She apparently hasn't eaten for some time, and she is badly mal-nourished."

"The baby?" Vi asked fearfully.

"The baby is not in such good condition," Dr. Frazier said steadily. "I believe in being forthright, and I will not give you false hope. The baby is very ill. Her fever is high and her lungs are congested. I have sent for a physician who has more experience than I in treating very young infants, and I want his opinion before I make a final diagnosis. The good news is that the child is strong—stronger than her mother. Your cousin apparently made sure that her baby was fed by sacrificing her own health."

"So it is Virginia's child?" Vi asked.

"Indeed it is," Dr. Frazier replied, hiding her surprise at Vi's question. "A little girl. She's about three months old, I'd say."

Dr. Frazier smiled now. "I wish your cousin had known to come to us," she continued, "but she did everything she could for her baby. She is a willful young woman, I think."

"Yes, she is," Vi said.

"And her mother, Mrs. Conley, is equally stubborn?" Dr. Frazier questioned.

"Oh, yes," Vi said.

"That's good, because they will need their fighting spirit to get through this. I have already judged your aunt to be a skilled nurse. So if your cousin's fever continues to recede, she can probably be taken to your hotel tomorrow or the next day. But we must see how the baby progresses before moving her."

"What can I do for them?" Vi asked.

"You've already done what was most important. You got them out of that apartment and here to me. Mrs. Conley has told me something of what happened. She said that you made all the right decisions. She's very grateful to you."

Vi's dark eyes widened in surprise. "Aunt Louise said that?"

"She did," Dr. Frazier replied with a knowing smile. "I observed that expressing gratitude doesn't come easily to Mrs.

Violet's Turning Point

Conley. She can stay here with her daughter tonight. I live above the clinic, and I have an extra bedroom where your aunt will be comfortable. Now, would you like to see your cousin?"

"Is Virginia well enough?" Vi asked. "I thought she was delirious."

"Delirious?" the doctor said with a look of puzzlement. "Her fever is high, but she is not delirious. When she learned that you brought her here, she asked to speak to you. I'm going to give her a sleeping draft, so come see her now while she's still awake."

~

Vi felt nervous as she followed Dr. Frazier to a small bedroom at the rear of the large house. She didn't know what to expect. All she could think of was the thin, thin face, splotched with fever, and the hollow eyes she'd seen when Virginia answered the door to the squalid apartment.

The shades were closed in the little room at the back of the clinic, but Vi felt a faint breeze when she entered. The walls were a light but cheerful yellow. Pretty framed prints hung on the walls. It wasn't at all like a sick room, Vi thought, and as far from the dreary apartment as day from night.

Virginia lay on the bed. She wore a clean white nightdress and was covered with a soft white sheet. Louise stood over her, gently patting a damp cloth to her face and neck.

Virginia didn't seem to recognize Vi at first. Then her eyes lit up, and she said in a hoarse voice, "Thank you, Vi. Thank you for saving my baby."

Vi moved close and said, "You did that, Virginia. The doctor says you sacrificed yourself to keep the baby fed."

"I thought we would get well," Virginia said, tears welling in her eyes.

"And you will, dear," Louise said in a tone so warm and gentle that it startled Vi.

"Of course you will," Vi added assuringly. "Dr. Frazier says that as soon as your fever is down, you can come to the hotel, and we can care for you there."

"And my baby?" Virginia asked.

Vi didn't hesitate. "Dr. Frazier says she is a strong baby and that you took very good care of her. Tell me about her."

A small smile came to Virginia's face, and suddenly she didn't look as ill as she really was. "She's the most beautiful baby. And not at all fussy. Oh, I . . ." Her voice broke, and Vi was afraid that she'd caused her cousin more sorrow.

But Louise caressed her daughter's cheek and said, "You were a very good baby, too. Your Papa called you his sweet little Ginny. He would be very proud of you and how strong you've been for your own little girl. Now, tell Vi how old she is."

The smile came back as Virginia said, "She's three months and five days old. She was born on the Ides of March — March the fifteenth. People say that's an unlucky day, but it was the best day of my life because she arrived."

Virginia lifted her hand, and Vi took it. Virginia said in a near-whisper, "I didn't know what love was until I held her in my arms. All the bad things just disappeared."

At this moment, Dr. Frazier entered. She carried a thermometer, a stethoscope, and a small brown bottle of medicine.

"That's enough conversation for now," the doctor said briskly. "I want to check my patient before she sleeps."

"May I ask my cousin just one question?" Vi said, looking to the doctor.

"If it's quick," Dr. Frazier said as she placed the stethoscope around her neck.

Turning back to Virginia, Vi said, "When we were leaving the apartment, you repeated one word again and again. Do you remember what it was?"

"I do," Virginia replied. "It was her name, my baby's name. Her name is Elizabeth, but I always call her Betsy. I was saying 'Betsy'."

"It's a beautiful name," Vi said.

⁓

In the hallway, Vi leaned against the wall to brace herself. Her knees were shaking, and she felt almost dizzy. The name ran through her head—Betsy, Betsy.

I heard it wrong, Vi thought. *I thought Virginia was saying "bed" or "bedside." But she was calling for Betsy, her baby.*

"Oh, dear Father in Heaven, thank You, thank You!" She prayed in a soft whisper. "I heard 'bed,' and I went back and found the baby. If I hadn't misunderstood, I might not have gone back. I might have thought Virginia really was delirious. We would have left the baby behind. But You took me to her! Even when I was wrong, You led me in the right way! You must want Virginia's baby to survive. Please, dear Lord, watch over her and make her well. I've asked You for a good deal of late, but this is so important. Please, bless Virginia and little Betsy with Your healing grace. I know that You are with them now. Please, if it is Your will, give Virginia and Aunt Louise and the baby this chance to love one another so they may receive Your gift of love and hope. Make them strong for each other. Please, give them life so that they may know You, Lord, and live with You always."

CHAPTER

7

Deceptions and Truths

*For there is nothing hidden that will
not be disclosed, and nothing
concealed that will not be
known or brought out
into the open.*

LUKE 8:17

Deceptions and Truths

A little more than a week had passed since Vi and Louise rescued Virginia and her baby. Virginia was making excellent progress, though she was still weak. Little Betsy's recovery was slower, but after several tense days, her fever had finally broken, and both Dr. Frazier and the consulting doctor pronounced her well enough to return to her mother at the hotel.

A room adjoining Louise's had been secured for Virginia and the baby. The consultant, Dr. Graves, continued to attend them, and a nurse was hired. The nurse—a highly skilled woman with a jolly manner and an even temperament—occasionally joked that she had too little work to justify her wages. Mrs. Conley and Mrs. O'Flaherty, she said, were as good at nursing as anyone trained for the job. But the nurse's presence gave Louise the hours she needed for sleep and, as it turned out, contemplation.

One morning when she was feeling stronger, Virginia asked her mother and Vi to come to her room. She wanted to tell them what had occurred in New York and why they'd found her in such miserable circumstances. Vi at first thought that she should not hear such private matters. But Virginia wanted her cousin to know.

"I've learned the terrible consequences of keeping secrets," Virginia said. "I was deceived, and to hide my shame, I deceived others. If I'm to be a good mother to my child, I must be honest with my mother and all my family. I have to start my life again with the truth."

It took some time to tell the story, and it is impossible to count the tears that were shed as she spoke.

Violet's Turning Point

Virginia began with her arrival in New York. When she and her new husband had moved there after their wedding, things had seemed fine at first. They lived in a nice apartment in a good neighborhood. Mr. Neuville introduced Virginia to his friends, who seemed more than acceptable. But it was not long before Virginia began to suspect that Mr. Neuville and his friends were not what they appeared to be.

Mr. Neuville's "financial business" turned out to be gambling and, Virginia had later learned, fraudulent business schemes. In the end, she had to admit that he had no real love for her; he had married her because he believed she had wealth. But she loved him, and she was determined to help him change his dishonest ways.

Their life did change, though not as Virginia hoped. Mr. Neuville made many promises to stop gambling and give up his "friends." But unknown to his wife, he was gambling even more recklessly and falling deeper and deeper into debt. They were forced to move from their nice apartment to a smaller one in a less prosperous area of the city. That was the first of many moves.

There had never been an elegant townhouse or rich friends or a gay social life. Virginia had manufactured these fantasies in every letter she wrote to her mother. They were all desperate lies, Virginia admitted with great remorse, but she had done it so that her mother would not be disappointed in her.

The Neuvilles had lived in increasingly depressed circumstances. What money Mr. Neuville made from his schemes, he lost at the gambling tables. To earn enough for their rent and food, Virginia had eventually found employment with Mrs. Vangelt, using the name Virginia Newman.

She had been working at the house near Gramercy Park for almost a year when she wrote her last letter to her mother. But by that time, she knew that she was going to have her baby, and Mr. Neuville, on learning of the pregnancy, had deserted her. He took almost everything of value and disappeared.

Virginia continued working until she could no longer hide her condition. Then she had lived alone until the baby was born, managing as long as she could on her meager savings. She sold what little she had—the last of her beautiful wedding clothes and the few jewels her husband had overlooked when he abandoned her. But the money went quickly. On the very day that Vi and Louise found her, Virginia had spent the last of it on milk for the baby. She had nothing left for rent and nowhere to go.

It was very difficult for Virginia to confess all this. She took full responsibility for her own part in her unhappiness and begged her mother's forgiveness for the lies. To Vi's amazement, Louise said that the fault was her own. She had pushed Virginia to marry a rich man. She had been completely dazzled by Mr. Neuville's handsome appearance, fine manners, and pretense of wealth. So she never bothered to investigate the man and his background. Not until Virginia failed to respond to her letters had she begun to worry. Even then, Louise hadn't allowed herself to think that Virginia might be in trouble.

"I have not been a good mother to you," Louise admitted when she had heard Virginia's full story. Her voice choked with powerful emotions, she said, "I deceived myself by thinking that you were being thoughtless and cruel. How could I have been so blind? It was the blindness of arrogance. I cared only that I be in the right. But I have been so wrong for so many years. It is you who must forgive me, my darling—if you can. I will spend the rest of my life making amends to you and my grandchild."

"We must both make amends," Virginia replied through her tears. "Oh, Mamma, I really need you! And Betsy needs you! Can we come home with you? Back to Roselands?"

Louise took Virginia in her arms. They cried together and after some moments, Louise began to laugh in a shy way. Laughter was not something she often allowed herself, and both Virginia and Vi regarded her with astonishment. Virginia asked, "Why are you laughing, Mamma?"

"Because I feel full of joy for the first time in so many years," Louise said. "Because God has blessed me, though I do not deserve it. We will go home together, and we will give little Betsy all the love that a child needs. Many years ago, I thought God had abandoned me. I see now that I abandoned Him. But He never gave up on me. He has brought you back to me and given me this opportunity to redeem myself. I'm laughing because I was foolish and arrogant and blind, and all this time, God never stopped loving me. I have a great many sins to make up for, but with His help, I will. I promise, dear child, that I will be a real mother to you and grandmother to Betsy."

Louise's words almost took Vi's breath away. Her own tears of joy began to flow. She had to gulp for air.

Louise turned to her and held out her hand. "Will you forgive me, Violet?" she asked. "Will you forgive my hard words and cruel judgments?"

Vi went to her aunt and grasped her hand. "I've made judgments, too, Aunt Louise. I've been impatient with you and not as respectful as I should be."

"Respect has to be earned, child," Louise said. She was still smiling, and her face looked years younger. "I have to earn your respect, Violet, and with God's help, I hope that I can."

"You've let God into your heart," Vi said, brushing the tears from her cheeks. "That's what matters."

"I've been praying," Louise said softly. "God has been speaking to me all along; yet for twenty years, I refused to listen. He has been with me every moment, offering to be my friend and my comfort. As a child and a girl, I went to church. I never paid much attention, but something must have penetrated my selfish heart. When I prayed for Virginia and the baby, it was as if I were coming home. I remembered part of a verse—'If you seek him, he will be found by you. . . .' It's true, Violet! All I had to do was open my heart, and I found Him!"

"Oh, it is true, Aunt Louise," Vi said. "And He will never desert you. The verse you remembered is from 1 Chronicles. King David tells his son Solomon, 'Acknowledge the God of your father, and serve him with wholehearted devotion and with a willing mind, for the LORD searches every heart and understands every motive behind the thoughts.'"

Virginia shifted against her pillow, and Louise helped her to sit up. "It had to be God who brought you both to me," Virginia said. "I wish I knew the Bible as well as you, Vi. But I will learn, and I'll teach Betsy. All the answers are there, aren't they?"

"We will learn it together," Louise said, hugging Virginia gently. "And we'll teach your darling Betsy as King David taught his son."

Vi excused herself and hurried back to her own room. From her bedside table, she took her little Bible. Returning quickly to Virginia's room, she handed the book to her aunt.

"Everything is here," she said. "It's God's Word, and it will never fail you."

"But where do we begin?" Virginia asked.

"You can begin anywhere," Vi replied. "The Bible is unlike any book that ever was or ever will be written, for God is in every word on every page. And every word is a new beginning."

Louise had opened the book at random to the first chapter of the book of John. She looked up at Vi with an expression of amazement. Then Louise read: "In the beginning was the Word, and the Word was with God, and the Word was God."

Virginia placed her thin hand over the page and said, "He has shown us where to start, Mamma. Please stay and read to me for a while."

"Have you noticed the changes in your aunt?" Zoe asked Vi as they were taking a walk in the park late the next morning. "I've seen her smiling quite often these past few days. She doesn't seem to resent Mrs. O anymore. They have long talks, and I hear them laughing together. Mrs. Conley is so good with the baby. Plus, she hasn't yelled at me in a whole week!"

"She is changing," Vi replied, "and it goes much deeper than what anyone can see. She has given her sadness and misery to our Lord. Remember how Mrs. O said that ice cracks under pressure? Well, the ice in Aunt Louise's heart is breaking up and melting away. She has let God in, and His love is warming her. She's smiling with a joy from inside. She's letting go of all the pain and resentment."

Zoe thought about this as they walked. Finally she asked, "Do you think it is a real change?"

"I do," Vi said. "Aunt Louise thought Virginia and the baby might die. After all the years of trying to make everyone do what she wanted—what she had decided was right—Aunt Louise was helpless. We all knew she was afraid, but we didn't realize how desolate she was. She turned to God in desperation, and He enfolded her in His love."

"It's like a miracle, isn't it?" Zoe said softly.

"God's healing love is the greatest miracle," Vi said.

They walked some distance in companionable silence before Vi turned her thoughts to practical matters. She asked, "What time are we expected at the Despards' today?"

"Four o'clock," Zoe said. "It's going to be a high tea, like in England, so there will be ever so much delicious food. I'm so glad you can go, Vi. If I'd known what you were doing last week, that you'd found Virginia and were at the clinic, I'd never have gone to tea with Mrs. Despard. But I didn't know, and I'm glad I saw her again. She's very sweet to me, and she knows the most interesting people."

"I'm also glad you saw her," Vi said. "I believe that Mrs. Despard has a high opinion of you."

"Really?" Zoe said. "I thought she was just being nice because of her and her husband's regard for Ed."

Vi stopped on the graveled path and looked at her friend. A little sternly, she said. "They like *you*, Zoe. They like you because you are bright and charming and fun to be with. And don't you go thinking otherwise."

Zoe flushed with pleasure. "That's very nice to hear," she said.

"It's nice because it's true," Vi said, and she began walking again.

Violet's Turning Point

As they strolled back to the hotel, the girls chatted happily about what they would wear to the Despards'. Zoe had received several of her new day-dresses, and this was to be her first occasion to go out in something other than her black mourning clothes.

They discussed other plans for their holiday. Now that Zoe had completed most of her shopping, she was anxious to see the museums, and Vi suggested some additional sites that they should visit. They had been invited to tea with Mrs. Vangelt, and they would attend the opera as the guests of Mr. and Mrs. Phillips. (Vi was very glad she hadn't had to contact Mr. Phillips for help in finding Virginia.)

"I still have a few things to buy," Zoe said, "but Mrs. O'Flaherty will go with me. I know how you feel about shopping."

"What else could you possibly need?" Vi laughed. "From the number of boxes in your room and the trunk we've already shipped back to Ion, I'd say that the shops of New York must all have bare shelves by now."

"Oh, there are a few things I haven't acquired," Zoe said with a smug little smile. "You wouldn't be interested."

"You make it sound like a mystery," Vi noted.

"Well, you know that I like mysteries," Zoe said. "I was looking forward to solving the mystery of Virginia, but you did it first. Still, I think I would make a very good detective if I had a case to solve. Maybe I can find some kind of secret mission."

Vi couldn't help giggling. "You couldn't keep it a secret," she said. "You're one of the most open and honest people I know, Zoe. However could you have a secret mission if you can't keep a secret?"

Zoe scrunched her eyebrows together in a fake frown. "I might surprise you, Vi," she said. "I might be on a deep, dark secret mission this very minute."

Looking at the little watch pinned to her jacket, Vi said, "Speaking of minutes, we must hurry. Mrs. O is meeting us for lunch at noon. Can you delay your secret mission long enough to eat?"

"Good detectives never miss their lunch." Zoe laughed as she skipped ahead a few steps.

CHAPTER

8

Pleasant Diversions

I was a stranger and you invited me in.

MATTHEW 25:35

Pleasant Diversions

*L*ouise made a point to speak to the girls before they departed for Marguerite Despard's tea. Zoe was wearing a new, rosy-hued silk dress with delicate lace trim at the neckline and on the sleeves. Her small hat was of the same pink material with a white feather attached jauntily to its side. Vi had chosen a crisp, light blue linen dress and a charming straw hat trimmed in silk flowers. Louise kissed them both and said, "You look like summer flowers. I doubt there are two prettier young ladies in New York today." Her kisses and compliments were a little stiff, but she was learning, and Vi felt blessed by her aunt's display of affection.

Mr. Meriweather, who had taken a special interest in the family of ladies from the South, was waiting to drive the girls to the Despard residence. As they neared the house, Vi realized that it was just a block or two from the Vangelt home—a very exclusive neighborhood. She couldn't help but compare these surroundings to the area where Virginia had been forced to live. She thought again of the shabby rooms the Constanza family had occupied in Rome. The contrast between those who had so much and those who had so little troubled her—as it always did—and she thought about Dr. Frazier and her clinic.

The carriage stopped before a brownstone house located on a corner. The house had a garden that ran across its front and down its side. A high iron fence separated the garden from the street, and tall hedges grew just inside the fence, providing privacy. Mr. Meriweather helped the girls to the sidewalk and said he would return in two hours. He got back onto his seat but waited until the girls were inside the house before he left. He smiled to himself, thinking how much Miss Zoe reminded him of his own eldest daughter.

A butler showed them into the parlor where Marguerite Despard greeted them gaily. There were a number of handsomely dressed men and women sitting and standing about the elegant, high-ceilinged room. Mrs. Despard made introductions, and Vi tried very hard to remember the names. She was hoping that Dr. Frazier might be there but didn't see her.

"Come out to the patio now, girls," Mrs. Despard said. "There are several of my guests there who want to see our Southern friends."

She led them through a wide set of glass side doors that opened onto a small, stone courtyard surrounded by fragrant plantings and flowering bushes.

Dr. Amelia Frazier was sitting on an iron bench, and two men were chatting with her. One was a tall, handsome man of about forty. His clothing was immaculate, and he was stylish in a way that made Vi guess he might be a European. The other man was short and wide and round-faced. He was dressed in brown from head to foot, and he seemed uncomfortable with the fragile teacup he was holding.

"You know my sister," Mrs. Despard said. "I would like you to meet Monsieur Alphonse, who has just arrived from France and will be our guest for several weeks. And this is Mr. Biggs, who is Monsieur Alphonse's business associate. Gentlemen, this is Miss Violet Travilla and Miss Zoe Love."

Monsieur Alphonse smiled warmly and said, "It is a great pleasure to meet such charming young ladies." His English was nearly perfect, though his accent was strong.

Mr. Briggs mumbled, "Pleased to meet you," in a flat American tone. These were the only words he spoke, and as the small group began conversing, he seemed to fade into the background.

A waiter came with tea for Vi and Zoe, and he informed Mrs. Despard that another guest had arrived. She excused herself.

Monsieur Alphonse addressed Zoe. "Our hostess tells me that you have only recently come here from Rome. I hope you are enjoying your stay as much as I am liking my visit to the United States."

"I am very much, sir, but I am not a visitor," Zoe replied. "I live now with Miss Travilla and her family in the South."

Dr. Frazier explained, "Miss Love's father was a diplomat, and she was raised in Europe."

"I grew up in Paris," Zoe added. "Then we lived in Rome until my father died."

Monsieur Alphonse's eyebrows went up, and Vi thought she saw something like surprised concern in his face. But it was gone in an instant.

"I am very sorry to hear of your loss," he said. "But you must tell me more of your life in Europe."

Zoe began to talk brightly about her years in Paris and Rome, and the monsieur listened carefully. He asked questions and seemed genuinely interested in her responses.

Meanwhile, Vi had joined Dr. Frazier on the bench and was answering her questions about Virginia and the baby.

Hearing that all was going well, Dr. Frazier said, "You were certainly the last person I expected to see at the clinic, but I am glad you remembered it. Our hospitals do their best, but I fear your cousin and her baby would not have fared so well there."

"Why is that?" Vi asked with interest.

"Except for the private facilities that serve the wealthy," the doctor said, "the hospitals are overcrowded and their staffs overworked. You might not have seen a doctor for hours. As it was, time was on our side. We were able to attend to your cousin and her daughter before either of them developed pneumonia."

Vi said, "I hoped you might be here today so that I could thank you again. But I didn't expect to see you."

Dr. Frazier smiled, and Vi realized again how pretty she was. Lowering her voice, the doctor said, "To be honest, I cannot stand these tea parties. I make an occasional appearance to please my sister, but I am a fish out of water here. Still, these gatherings are necessary for Marguerite's work for the museum."

At Vi's puzzled look, the doctor explained, "The museum relies on the support of people with the money and time to care about art. They must be entertained and pampered if they are to be generous. Marguerite introduces wealthy New Yorkers to people like Monsieur Alphonse who know about art. The wealthy become educated about the city's need for cultural institutions. Marguerite and I are not so different really. I want to improve the health of the city, and she strives to raise its spirit."

"I would like to know more about your work," Vi said. "I — I have an idea of what I want to do with my life." She lowered her eyes shyly and went on, "I want to help people in need, but I have much to learn about the right way to serve."

Dr. Frazier studied Vi's face for a few moments. Then she said, "If you are really interested, I would like you to visit the clinic again. When would you care to come?"

"Oh, anytime," Vi said, looking up with a wide smile. "That is, anytime that is convenient for you. I don't want to be in your way."

"I will put you to work," the doctor said with a little laugh. "Do you have any experience with children?"

"I have four younger brothers and sisters," Vi said. "I teach Sunday school, and I once spent several days helping with the children at a mission and clinic in New Orleans. Does that count?"

"Indeed it does. Well, could you come tomorrow afternoon at about three?"

"Yes, thank you, Dr. Frazier," Vi said. "Tomorrow at three would be wonderful."

Marguerite Despard had returned to the group just in time to hear her sister's invitation.

"So you have found a new recruit, Amelia," she said.

"An interested observer," Dr. Frazier corrected. "Miss Travilla is seeing your work today, and tomorrow she will see mine."

"Well, I must get back to my work," Mrs. Despard whispered. She turned to Monsieur Alphonse and Zoe. "I have to steal you away, Francois. Mrs. Longley has come and is most anxious to discuss a new acquisition for the Renaissance art gallery."

"Ah," Monsieur Alphonse smiled knowingly. "The lady whose husband builds the railroads. Please excuse me, Mademoiselle Love. Perhaps we may speak again later."

"That would be very nice, Monsieur," Zoe said with a little curtsey.

He bowed to all the ladies and followed Mrs. Despard into the house. Trotting just behind was the little Mr. Biggs.

"Monsieur Alphonse is ever such a nice man," Zoe said as she dropped down onto a chair beside the bench where Vi and the doctor sat. "He knew my father in Paris. I'm not exactly sure how. Probably through some diplomatic thing. Do you know Monsieur Alphonse, Dr. Frazier?"

"I just met him today," the doctor said. "I know that he is a dealer in art and that he is very suave. But I can't help wondering about his associate, the little man in brown. He doesn't seem like an art dealer. In fact, he reminds me of a policeman."

"But policemen wear uniforms, don't they?" Zoe asked.

"Not all of them," Dr. Frazier said. "There are detectives who dress in suits like businessmen."

Vi had to laugh. "There, Zoe, you may have found a detective. Perhaps he can tell you how mysteries are solved."

"Maybe he's on a secret mission," Zoe giggled.

"I think he would be quite good at keeping secrets," said Dr. Frazier, enjoying the girls' conversation. "Since he never seems to talk, he couldn't tell what he knew."

A familiar voice interrupted them as Mr. Despard came out the door.

"It's so nice to see our young friends again," he was saying in his hearty manner. "You must come in and sample the food. Marguerite and the cook have outdone themselves."

He ushered them into the dining room, where guests were standing around the table. An older lady was pouring tea from a silver urn. She wore a tight black lace dress and so much jewelry around her neck and on her ears that Vi wondered how she held her head up.

"That's Mrs. Longley," Dr. Frazier whispered. "She is a great admirer of Queen Victoria and always wears black, though unlike the Queen's late husband, Mrs. Longley's husband is very much alive. She loves to preside at events like this. I believe I could feed a hundred families for a hundred years for the price of the diamonds she's wearing."

Zoe stifled a giggle, but Vi realized that Dr. Frazier was only half-joking. They got their food and fresh cups of tea. It was all quite splendid—the food, the conversation, the beautiful house, which was filled with works of art. Mr. and Mrs. Despard went out of their way to make Vi and Zoe feel comfortable.

When it was time to leave, Mrs. Despard accompanied the girls to the door.

"My sister had to depart early," she told Vi. "She made me promise to remind you. Three o'clock at the clinic. Since you will be with Amelia, perhaps Zoe might visit me tomorrow afternoon."

To Zoe, she said, "I'm going to the museum, and I'd like you to come. I can get you at the hotel after lunch. We'll see the exhibit, and then you can come back with me and have supper. No party. Just a few friends."

Zoe looked at Vi, and Vi nodded. Mrs. Despard kissed both girls on their cheeks and waved them farewell as Mr. Meriweather saw them safely inside his carriage and drove away.

Back at the hotel, Zoe excitedly told Mrs. O'Flaherty about all the interesting people they had met. But Vi excused herself and went to her room. She wanted to write a letter to her mother. She wrote to Elsie almost every day—and nearly as frequently to Ed—and she had received many helpful and encouraging letters in return.

She was just finishing her letter when Zoe knocked at her door and came in.

"Mrs. O says she'll be ready for dinner in a half hour," Zoe said. "I'm glad we're eating late. I had so much at the Despards that I need a little time to work up my appetite again."

Violet's Turning Point

Vi smiled at her friend and said, "You always have an appetite. I never knew a girl who enjoyed food so much."

Zoe plopped down on Vi's bed and said, "My Papa always said that food is a kind of art to be appreciated. He said it's not just the taste we should appreciate, but all the hard work that goes into the preparation. He said food can be like music, that it takes many talented hands working together to create a great meal."

She rolled onto her stomach and propped her chin on her hands. "Did you know that Mrs. O's husband was a musician?" she asked.

Vi was sealing her letter as she said, "Yes. He taught piano and composed music, but his work was never performed. Mrs. O also taught piano."

"It must be very sad," Zoe said wistfully, "to work so hard on creating music and never get the chance to have other people hear it. It's like cooking a feast and then having no one eat it."

"There must have been a reason why Mr. O'Flaherty's work wasn't performed," Vi said.

"Mrs. O says it was because his compositions were ahead of their time," Zoe replied. She rolled over and sat up, dangling her feet over the side of the bed. "Do you know that she keeps his music with her always?"

Vi didn't know this and said so.

"She keeps all his compositions in that old valise of hers," Zoe explained. "When we were shopping one day, I asked if she'd like a new valise, since hers has a broken handle and is just tied up with string. That's when she told me about the music and how she brought it with her when she came to the United States. She lived here in New York for a couple of years and worked as a housekeeper because it paid better than teaching piano. But all the while she was trying to show her husband's music to people who might help. She said that several musicians were interested, but she could never meet anyone in a position to make a decision. If the music was to be performed, it needed a sponsor—like an orchestra conductor or a famous performer. But she was just a housekeeper. How could she meet a famous person like that?"

Most of this information was new to Vi.

"But is she still hopeful?" Vi asked.

"I think she has given up trying," Zoe said with a sad shake of her head. "She said that her husband's work is still ahead of its time. But she will keep it always and see that it is passed on to someone who can try again after she's gone."

"Gone?"

"She meant after she dies. She is sure his music is great, and she believes that somewhere, sometime, someone will discover it and present it for the world to hear. Don't you think that's romantic?"

"It's an act of true love," Vi said softly. "I wonder if Mamma could help. Maybe she could show the music to someone important."

"Oh, that's ever such a good idea," Zoe exclaimed. "I don't believe Mrs. O would want to impose on your mother, but *you* could! Ask, I mean, not impose."

"But let's not say anything to Mrs. O yet," Vi said. "I don't want to disappoint her if Mamma cannot do anything. If she can help, then she should be the one who speaks to Mrs. O."

Zoe readily agreed. Then she asked, "Do you think the music might really be good?"

Vi considered for a few seconds, then said, "Mrs. O thinks so, and I trust her judgment. And I'm sure that Mamma will know if she can see the music."

"Your mother is a musician?" Zoe asked.

"A very good one," Vi said with pride. "She studied piano for many years with excellent teachers. She plays beautifully, but not so often now. Missy inherited her talent."

"I know how talented your sister is," Zoe said. "Missy played for us in Rome, and Papa said she could be a professional. Are you musical too?"

Vi laughed. "I wish I were," she said. "I took lessons, but Papa said I was like him. Our real talent was for the appreciation of music played by others."

"I'm not musical at all," Zoe said without any regret. "But I like it—especially singing. Papa always took me to the opera. What does one wear to the opera in New York?"

They began talking about clothes. They were discussing their plans for the last two weeks of their visit when Mrs. O'Flaherty opened the door.

"Am I interrupting you two?" she asked.

"Not at all," Zoe said. "Are you ready for dinner?"

"I'm quite hungry," Mrs. O'Flaherty replied. "But after your tea at Mrs. Despard's, I'm sure you will want only a bit of bread and perhaps some weak tea."

Zoe giggled. "Actually I was thinking about roast chicken and some delicious vegetables. And chocolate cake for dessert. Or custard tart with fresh strawberries. Or . . ."

They were still laughing about Zoe's appetite when they entered the hotel dining room a few minutes later.

CHAPTER

9

The Clinic

*He who is kind to the poor lends
to the LORD, and he will
reward him for what
he has done.*

PROVERBS 19:17

The Clinic

*V*i arrived at the clinic precisely at three o'clock the next afternoon, and Dr. Frazier met her at the door. Vi could hardly hear the doctor's greeting for the sounds of children laughing and shouting.

"I meant it when I said that I'd put you to work," Dr. Frazier said above the din. "Mrs. Giannelli has brought her entire family. Little Marco is ill, but as you can hear, the other seven are perfectly healthy. If you could read to them, it might lower the noise so that I can hear myself think. There's a cupboard in the waiting room, and the books are on the top shelf."

Vi was soon introduced to the Giannelli children. Their mother told them to line up, and from the youngest to the eldest, they made perfect stair steps. Vi shook each hand and learned each name. Then she asked if they enjoyed stories. At a chorus of yeses, she said she would select a book if the children would sit in a little alcove she had spotted.

"You can sit in a circle on the floor," she said, "and save a place for me."

The children were surprised that the pretty young lady would sit with them, but they did as Vi suggested. She quickly rummaged through the books in the cupboard and selected one that she thought would appeal to all.

Seating herself, she showed them the book. "Have you ever heard the story of *The Emperor's New Clothes*?" she asked.

A couple of the older children nodded, and Vi held up the book so the children could see the picture of the Emperor surrounded by the people in his court. Then she read.

The children were all laughing when she finished.

A little boy of about six giggled, "The Emperor musta looked silly, walking around in his underwear." His remark brought another round of laughs.

A girl, whom Vi guessed to be nine or ten years old, said, "I like that story because it's funny and it has a lesson too. It's about having the courage to tell the truth even when everybody else won't. The child told the truth."

"Jesus told stories like that," commented one of her older sisters. "In the Bible, His parables teach us how to live and do what's right."

Vi asked, "Do you all study the Bible?"

The girl smiled shyly and replied, "Yes, ma'am. It's the only book in our house, and our Mamma reads it to us every night. She says it's the most important book ever written."

"Your mother is correct," Vi said with a warm smile. Then she asked, "Do you all have favorite Bible stories?"

Immediately the children broke into a babble of answers: "Joseph in his coat!" "David and Goliath!" "The baby Jesus!"

Laughing, Vi held up her hands and said, "Wait! I can't understand when you all talk at once. Let's go around the circle, and one by one, you can tell me your favorites. But let's not shout because that makes it very hard for Dr. Frazier to do her work."

The children calmed instantly, and each spoke in turn. Vi made a point to ask every child a question or two, and the children were clearly pleased by her interest.

They were talking quietly when a loud commotion at the front door interrupted them. A man was yelling at the clinic nurse, "Get the doctor! This child's been badly hurt!"

The Clinic

Vi turned to see a tall man in a police uniform. He was carrying a young boy. The boy lay limp in the man's arms. The boy's face was deathly pale, and he was obviously unconscious. A blood-soaked cloth was wrapped around one of his arms and his chest.

The Giannelli children all gasped in horror, and Vi told them to stay seated. The youngest boy crawled to her, and she took him in her lap. The other children moved closer to her, breaking their circle and becoming a tight huddle around her. They were frightened, but not even the smallest one cried.

Soothingly she said, "We must all be very quiet now. That's how we can help."

Dr. Frazier had come running into the room, and she led the policeman through a curtained door near the back of the clinic. Vi could hear urgent voices from behind the curtain but couldn't make out what was said. Then she saw that several other men were standing in the entryway. The nurse came and talked to them. After some minutes, the men went outside again.

There were only a few other people waiting for the doctor, and the nurse spoke to them, explaining that the doctor would have to see them later. Then she came to Vi and the terrified children.

In a brisk but kindly way, the nurse said, "There was an accident at the laundry. The doctor is attending to it. Children, your mother is just coming. Your baby brother will be fine. You wait right here for your mother." Then she hurried away and disappeared behind the curtain.

The girl who had spoken about Jesus' parables whispered to Vi. "It's Michael," she said. "The boy who's hurt. He used to go to school with me, but he left. He works in the laundry. People are always getting hurt there."

"But how old is he?" Vi asked.

"'Bout twelve, I guess," the girl said. "He lives with his grandmother, I think, over on Becker Street."

Mrs. Giannelli, with young Marco in her arms, appeared at that moment, and the children all rushed to her.

"Thank you, Miss, for watching over my babies," Mrs. Giannelli said as she hustled her children to the door and out of the clinic.

Vi didn't know what to do next. She rose from the floor. She looked around. All but one of the people waiting to see the doctor had left when Mrs. Giannelli did. Only an elderly lady remained.

Vi went to the long wooden bench where the old woman sat.

"Would ya like a seat?" the woman said.

"No, but thank you," Vi replied. "I need to stretch my legs after sitting so long."

"I noticed. You're good with them children," the woman commented. Her voice was rough and betrayed little emotion as she continued, "I had children once. Lost two of my boys in work accidents. That was twenty years ago, and things ain't got any better, have they? Poor folks work and die so rich folks can be happy."

This last remark shocked Vi and tore at her heart. "But surely the boy won't die," she said in disbelief.

"Maybe. Maybe not," the woman said. "But he'll most likely lose that arm. Then he can't work, and that's as good as dead when you're poor. I know. I've seen it too many times. It's worse than a war how many children die just trying to earn a few pennies for their families. But we can pray for him. Shut your eyes, girl, and pray for God to have mercy on that child."

The Clinic

Vi closed her eyes and prayed in silence, earnestly asking her Heavenly Father to help the boy and to guide Dr. Frazier. *Please touch the lives of all the children, dear Lord, so they can put their hope in You and know Your love.* Then she added, *Help me, too, to know what I can do to serve them. Help me to find the path that You want me to follow. Amen.* When she looked up, the nurse was handing a brown bottle to the old woman and saying, "The doctor wants you to take two tablespoons of this tonight and two in the morning. It should settle your stomach. But if you still can't eat, come back tomorrow, and the doctor will see you first thing."

The old woman mumbled something, and stood. The nurse took her arm and assisted her to the door.

"She'll be back tomorrow," the nurse said when the woman was gone. "Nothing much wrong with her except loneliness. We get a lot like her—women who've outlived their husbands and children and friends. Dr. Frazier is very kind to them, but when there's a real emergency, like that boy in there, she has to put first things first."

"How is the boy?" Vi asked.

"Not good. His arm is crushed and his shoulder's broken. He got caught in one of those giant presses. He has to go to the hospital. Dr. Frazier has sent for an ambulance."

"Do you think he'll survive?"

"He might, but sometimes dying is not the worst that can happen," the nurse said with a sad shake of her head. Resuming her professional tone, she added, "Dr. Frazier asked if you wanted to wait for her. But she thought you might prefer to return at another time."

Vi said, "I'd like to stay, but I'm sure the doctor will be tired."

The nurse smiled, "I think she'd like to have some company. I'm going to close up and go home after the ambulance

arrives. The police officer will go to the hospital with the boy, so Dr. Frazier will be alone. These kinds of accident tend to get her down, so it would be good if you could stay for awhile. She might need someone to talk to."

"Of course, I'll stay," Vi said. "But do these accidents happen often?"

"Too often," the nurse replied. "It might be a man or a woman, but it's hardest when it's a child—though I don't guess that boy has had much chance to be a child. I wish we knew who he is."

"One of the Giannelli children said his name is Michael and he lives with his grandmother," Vi said. She struggled to remember what else the girl had told her. Then it came. "She said he lives on Baker—no, Becker Street."

The nurse smiled again and said, "Oh, that is a help! I'll tell the officer, and the police will find his family. Now you just sit here and wait. It shouldn't be too long."

❧

An hour later, Vi and Dr. Frazier were sitting in the small parlor of the doctor's apartment on the third floor of the clinic building. The ambulance had come and gone, taking the unconscious boy to the hospital. When Mr. Meriweather arrived to collect Vi, she'd told him that she'd be returning to the hotel in the doctor's carriage and given him a note to deliver to Mrs. O'Flaherty.

Dr. Frazier made tea, and now she was reclining with her feet up on a small couch. Vi sat on a larger sofa opposite. She looked around the parlor. It was simply furnished, but all the items in the room were of excellent quality. There were several landscape paintings on the walls, and Vi wanted to examine them more closely. A portrait of a young woman in a satin ball gown hung above the fireplace, and Vi guessed that it might be the doctor's mother because of the strong resemblance to Dr. Frazier.

Vi could see how tired the doctor was, but as they sipped their hot, sweet tea, Dr. Frazier seemed to relax.

"Will the boy be all right?" Vi asked. She was remembering what Dr. Frazier had said about the overcrowded hospitals that served the poor.

"He lost a great deal of blood," Dr. Frazier said. "His arm was nearly amputated by that wretched machine, and I am afraid the surgeons will not be able to save it. But I was able to control the bleeding. If he's not too weak, he may live, though that is not the same as being all right."

Vi dropped her eyes and said, "I'm so sorry. Who will care for him?"

"His grandmother perhaps, if she's strong enough. Some of the churches may be able to help. If I'm lucky, he will come back here, and we can assist him."

"But what of his employer—the laundry? Are they not responsible for him? It was their machine that caused the accident."

Dr. Frazier smiled in a way that was not happy. "In this country, businesses have no responsibility for their employees' health and well-being. That laundry is a dreadful place, but no different from other industries. They hire mostly new immigrants and young children and work them like dogs for earnings that cannot feed and clothe one person, much less a family. The machines they use are all unsafe, yet when a worker is injured or killed, the owners say that the worker is at fault. They will say that the boy was careless and that he caused the accident."

"Isn't there some kind of law?" Vi asked.

"Yes, there are laws," the doctor replied with a heavy sigh, "and they all favor the owners. That boy is not entitled to a penny's worth of assistance."

"But that has to be changed," Vi said with vehemence. "There can be no work without workers. The owners depend on their workers and should be responsible for their welfare."

"The problem is that there are always people ready to take the jobs," Dr. Frazier explained. "New immigrants arrive every day in New York and our other big cities. Many don't speak English. Most are fleeing poverty in their old countries and hoping for a better life here. There are some who are able to rise, but most find only more poverty and misery. They're forced to live in tenements and work at the lowest-paying jobs. When one is hurt or dies, there are probably a hundred ready to take his place. That poor boy will not even be missed, for tomorrow another boy will be doing the work he did today."

"I don't understand," Vi said. "At home, our workers are taken care of even when they can't work. There are people living at Ion who were slaves before my mother and father were born. They always have a home there, if they choose to stay. My father said that his employees were his greatest asset and that their work should be valued above everything else. He worked side by side with the farm hands whenever he could. That's how he died—working with the people he employed."

Dr. Frazier stared at Vi. "Truly?" she questioned.

"Oh, yes," Vi replied. "He always said that God made no distinction between people, that an employer was no different in God's eyes than a worker."

The Clinic

" 'But let justice roll on like a river, righteousness like a never-failing stream,' " Dr. Frazier said, quoting from the fifth chapter of Amos.

"Do you know that some people believe that poverty itself is a kind of justice," the doctor continued, "and that poor people cause their own suffering because they are lazy or stupid or criminal by nature? How can they forget our Lord's words in the book of Matthew? 'I tell you the truth, whatever you did not do for one of the least of these, you did not do for me,' " Dr. Frazier said with a sigh, and Vi heard the sadness in her tone.

"Surely not everyone believes that," Vi said questioningly. "What of the churches?"

"They do whatever they can," Dr. Frazier replied. "The congregations in this neighborhood have been wonderful, but you must remember that they are very poor, and their members spend almost every minute trying to feed and shelter their families. People will help their neighbors whenever they can, and I have seen many noble acts of self-sacrifice among the poor. But they can't make laws and change conditions."

Sitting up suddenly, Dr. Frazier placed her cup on a small table. She asked, "Are you interested in justice?"

"Yes, Dr. Frazier, when justice means doing what is right," Vi said. "But I know that justice can be twisted to benefit some people and harm others. That's what happened with slavery. The law said it was right, but it was wrong—unjust. And we had to fight a terrible war to end it."

Dr. Frazier smiled at Vi's comments and said, "You have a good deal of wisdom for a young woman of your tender years. If you truly want to serve the poor, you must be ready to recognize injustice and do battle with it. You will want to change everything, but you must be prepared to take small steps and earn small victories. Sometimes you will fail even in the small things. I warn you that it can be very discouraging. There will be times when you will suffer because, even with all your personal wealth and advantages, you can't achieve justice for others."

Vi realized that the doctor was now talking about herself, for Dr. Frazier was suffering as a result of the probable fate of the injured boy she had treated that day.

"I think I'm ready to face disappointments, Dr. Frazier," Vi replied thoughtfully. "I have the greatest example to follow — our Lord who left the riches of Heaven to become poor and to live on earth as a man, so that through His life we might share in His kingdom. I have His life to guide me in this world and His promise of an end of all suffering when this life is ended. God has promised in His Word that He Himself would help me."

Dr. Frazier's smile was full of warmth as she said, "Keep faith with His promise, and you will always find hope where others see failure. Think of all that He endured for our sakes, and it will relieve your own pain."

Then her whole face brightened as she said, "This conversation has made me feel much better. I knew you were an interesting young lady, Miss Travilla, and I hope we will be good friends. Now, may I call you Vi, and will you address me as Amelia? If we're going to be friends, then we must speak to one another as friends."

Amelia stood up and got the teapot from a side table. "Let's have one more cup before supper," she said. She poured the tea and sat down again, saying, "You have seen my clinic. Now I want to hear about your ideas for serving people in need."

The Clinic

So Vi began to explain her dream to open a mission for the poor. She told Amelia about her experience at the mission in New Orleans and the work that Reverend and Mrs. Carpenter were doing there. She described the situation in her own city and the conditions in the South, especially the treatment of former slaves and their families.

The doctor asked, "What services would you provide at your mission?"

"Whatever people need," Vi said.

"People need a great deal," said the doctor. "If you're serious, you have to focus on what you can do that will be the most help."

"Well, I think that education and medical care are probably the most important," Vi said.

"Then you would have a school?"

"Yes, and maybe a place for young children to come while their mothers and fathers are at work. I'd want to feed the children when they're there. I'd want to feed anyone who is hungry. And a clinic like yours. Plus —"

"Whoa!" Amelia said with a kindly laugh. "And how will you pay for all this? I know that your family has wealth, as does mine, but to succeed you will need financial support from others. You'll need expertise that you do not have for tasks you can't or don't want to do yourself. To run a mission or a school or a clinic means that you must be a business-woman and a manager. I learned that the hard way when I opened the clinic. I thought that I could just hang out my shingle and care for the sick. If it hadn't been for Chris, my brother-in-law, I would have failed within a year. He keeps the books and manages the money for me, but I've had to learn what is being done and why. There are always bills to be paid and financial decisions to be made, you know."

Violet's Turning Point

"I hadn't really thought about the business part," Vi admitted.

"I have no doubt you can learn what is needed," Amelia said. "You are smart and dedicated. But tell me, do you have a sense of humor?"

"Yes, I think so," Vi replied. "Is that important?"

"It is," Amelia said. "A person with a sense of humor is, I have observed, often a person with perspective. It's very important to be able to judge between what is essential and what is merely convenient. There are situations that you can't just fix as you would mend a broken lamp or a leaking faucet. Sometimes you have to be creative to solve a problem, and sometimes you have to admit to yourself that you cannot solve a problem. As I said before, you'll be defeated if you regard your disappointments as failures. To know what you can do and can't do takes perspective."

"I'm not sure what you mean," Vi said.

"Let me give you an example," Amelia said. "You met an old lady today. Her name is Mrs. Weaver and she's one of my favorite people. She was my first patient here, and I quickly discovered that she was in excellent health for her age. I told her that she didn't need to see me unless she was sick or hurt, but she kept coming back. At first, I thought I was wasting my time with her when others had real medical problems. But I didn't have the heart to turn her away, and as I got to know her, I began to understand how lonely she is. Her husband and her sons are all dead, and she has no other family. Mrs. Weaver is a woman of faith, but she lacked everyday contact with other people. She needed to talk, so I began to make time for her—time to listen. Then I discovered that I was looking forward to her visits. She helped me understand this neighborhood and how people here think. I realized that I can't *solve* her problems, but I can share my time with her and care about her as a person. That's what I mean by perspective."

Vi was thoughtful. She said, "Reverend Carpenter once told me that to serve the needs of others, a person has to listen and pay attention. He said you have to find out what people really need before you can help. That's what you did with Mrs. Weaver, wasn't it?"

"Yes, and that's also what she did for me. When I first came here, I thought that I would do all the helping. But this gruff old lady helped me by telling me, in her way, about what it's like to be poor. She helped me open my eyes to the reality of life for the people I serve. Before I met her, I was very serious about myself and my vocation. I'm still serious about my profession and always will be. But now I often laugh at myself. As you can probably tell, I have a tendency to be pompous and give advice to others."

She laughed, and Vi did too. Vi said, "But I need your advice, so please give me all that you have."

Amelia rose, saying, "Well, my advice now is that we retire to the kitchen and prepare our supper. I'm not a very good cook, so it will be simple fare. Do you cook?"

"Not really," Vi confessed.

"That is one of the disadvantages of growing up with privileges. Someone else always prepares the meals. I didn't know how to boil water until I was in medical college. What few kitchen skills I have are self-taught."

"So you advise me to learn cooking?" Vi asked.

"Most definitely," the doctor replied with an almost girlish grin. "If you want to help other people, you have to take good care of your own health. Nourish your body as you nourish your spirit. I hope you like vegetables."

"Everything except broccoli," Vi said.

In the kitchen, Amelia began rummaging through a large straw basket that sat on the table. "I see carrots and some baby potatoes and greens for salad. Oh, some fresh mushrooms, too. But no broccoli. You are fortunate tonight."

"I'll eat broccoli if I must," Vi said a little apologetically.

"Then you have perspective," Amelia said. "Broccoli is a problem you cannot eliminate, for there will always be broccoli. So you avoid it when you can and eat it when you must. Can you peel carrots?"

"I can peel them and I can eat them," Vi said playfully. "I just don't know how to cook them."

"The first step is to boil some water," Amelia said as she lit the stove. "All great ventures begin with small steps."

They had just finished eating when a bell rang in the apartment.

"Someone's at the front door," Amelia said. "I hope it's not another emergency."

"I'll come down with you," Vi said, thinking she might be able to assist if the doctor needed her.

They hurried down the two flights of stairs, and Amelia opened the front door. It was the policeman who had taken the boy to the hospital.

"Sorry to bother you, Dr. Frazier, but I wanted to tell you that the boy made it through the surgery. They couldn't save his arm, but they think he has a chance to live. They'll know better in a couple of days."

"Thank you very much, Sergeant Doyle," Amelia said. "You're very kind to let me know."

The Clinic

The officer seemed to have something else to say, but he hesitated. Seeing his discomfort, the doctor asked him to come inside.

"Thank you, ma'am, but I must be getting home," he replied. Then he went on, "There was one thing. The hospital wanted to know if someone would be paying for the boy. I said they should talk to you."

"That's good. I will go there tomorrow to make arrangements. I don't want that child in a charity ward," Amelia said firmly. "He's going to need full-time nursing. Did you find his family by chance?"

"Officer Finley did. There's just a grandmother, and she's too feeble to do nursing. Looks like the boy was supporting them both on his earnings. I have their address for you." He reached inside his jacket and took out a little notebook. He tore off a page and handed it to Amelia.

"Is there anything else I can do for you?" he asked.

Amelia said there was. She asked the sergeant if he could find a carriage for her guest, and he said he would have one at her door within fifteen minutes.

"I was going to drive you myself, Vi, but this will be quicker. It's been such a nice evening, but your family will worry if you aren't back soon. Will you visit me again? I didn't have time to show you everything about the clinic. Besides," she added with that smile that made her look like a girl, "now that I know how well you manage children, I am tempted to offer you a permanent position."

"I'd like that," Vi said, "but now that I know how important perspective is, I must use it. I'll come as often as you want me and learn as much as I can. Then I can take what I learn home—where it's needed."

"I like the way you think," the doctor said. "Come tomorrow if you can."

A Surprise Visitor

Humility and the fear of the
LORD bring wealth and
honor and life.

PROVERBS 22:4

A Surprise Visitor

Over breakfast the next morning, Vi told Zoe and Mrs. O'Flaherty all that had happened at the clinic and her plans to return that day. Then Zoe described her evening at the Despards'.

"It wasn't important like what you did at the clinic," Zoe said, "but it was ever so nice. Ed would have been proud of me. I didn't cause any spills."

"It's important that you enjoy yourself," Vi said. "That is why Mamma wanted you to have this holiday in New York. What would you like to do today?"

"Mrs. O and I thought we might take a ride on the elevated railway. Mrs. O says that the steam trains are very noisy, but I think it will be exciting to see the city from so many feet above the streets. Then we will visit the Astor Library. I understand that it is a remarkable place, with the largest collection of books in all America. It was built by one of your great millionaires, Mr. John Jacob Astor. After that, we have a little shopping to finish," Zoe added with a sly little smile.

"Another of your secret missions?" Vi joked.

"Oh, just the same old one," Zoe replied enigmatically.

Vi laughed. Then she inquired how Virginia and the baby were.

"They're both fattening up nicely," Mrs. O'Flaherty answered. "Virginia got up yesterday afternoon and was much more steady on her feet than I expected. With good food and plenty of rest, she's getting her strength back quickly now."

"And the baby smiled at me!" Zoe exclaimed. "I was holding her, and she gave me the most adorable grin. It's funny how sweet a baby's smile is even though she hasn't a tooth in her head."

Mrs. O'Flaherty continued, "Mrs. Conley received a letter from her son Cal. He and his brother Dr. Arthur are coming to New York to take them home. They'll be here in a couple of days. It's going to be a grand reunion for them all."

Back in their rooms, Zoe and Mrs. O'Flaherty quickly readied themselves for their excursion and were soon off. Vi looked in on Virginia and was very glad to see her up and dressed. Louise was cradling the baby in her arms and cooing to her like the happiest grandmother on earth. They visited for about an hour, and Vi was struck again and again by all the changes in her family.

She returned to her room and began a letter to her mother. It was a long letter, full of the clinic and Dr. Frazier and the injured boy. By the time she completed it, the clock stood at half past noon. She had to hurry in order to reach the clinic by one o'clock.

Zoe and Mrs. O'Flaherty returned to the hotel just as Vi was departing, and they crossed paths in the lobby.

"Would you like me to come with you?" Mrs. O'Flaherty asked Vi. "The clinic is in a dangerous part of town. I don't want to be a mother hen, but it might be safer if two of us go."

"No need to worry," Vi said. "I already have a mother hen. Mr. Meriweather isn't working today, but he arranged for another driver to take me wherever I want to go. His carriage is outside now, and he will bring me back in plenty of time for supper. So you and Zoe can do whatever you like"—she nodded at Zoe—"even more secret missions."

"I'm sure we can find something that doesn't involve secrets," said Mrs. O'Flaherty. "When should we expect you?"

"By six," Vi said as she rushed out the door.

A Surprise Visitor

After their morning of sightseeing, Zoe and Mrs. O'Flaherty completed one last errand at a shop not far away. Then they returned to the hotel for a late lunch, and Zoe went to see Virginia and play with the baby. Mrs. O'Flaherty invited Louise to take a walk in the park, and Louise agreed.

By three o'clock, Virginia and little Betsy were both napping, and Louise—invigorated by her walk—had gone to her room to write letters.

Zoe and Mrs. O'Flaherty were alone in the sitting room of the suite, talking about a special shopping task they had accomplished that day, when a bellman knocked at the door. He told them that a gentleman was downstairs and wished to see them. He handed a card to Mrs. O'Flaherty. She showed the card to Zoe, and then she instructed the doorman to tell the gentleman that they would receive him.

Not many minutes later, Monsieur Alphonse was sitting in a comfortable chair and apologizing graciously for stopping by without advance notice.

"I was at a gallery in the next block and remembered that you and Miss Travilla were staying at this hotel. I presumed to call," he said.

"Oh, it's nice that you did," Zoe replied. "Mrs. O'Flaherty has ordered tea, and you can join us."

"That is very kind of you," he said. "And I can hear about your impressions of the city."

Mrs. O'Flaherty had little to say at first. Zoe had talked in glowing terms about this Monsieur Alphonse, but Mrs. O'Flaherty wanted to judge for herself. He was certainly a handsome man, she thought. As the conversation proceeded, she realized that he was both well educated and widely traveled. She asked him a few questions about Paris that would be obscure to most people, and his answers were both knowledgeable and genuine. By the time tea arrived, she was feeling quite comfortable that the monsieur was indeed what he seemed—a charming French gentleman interested in the friendship of others who, like himself, were visitors to the city.

Zoe had no doubts at all. She chatted gaily—much as she had talked to her own father.

"So what do you think of the South?" Monsieur Alphonse asked. "It is very hot there, I have been told."

"This is just my first summer in America," Zoe replied. "Mrs. O'Flaherty knows the South better than I, for she has lived there for many years. She lived in Louisiana."

"Ah, as a Frenchman, I know of Louisiana," Monsieur Alphonse said. "Tell me, Mrs. O'Flaherty, how you came to this country? You are Irish, I think?"

"I am," Mrs. O'Flaherty replied. "But like Zoe, I lived in Paris and Rome for many years. My husband was a musician and teacher. When he died, I came to the United States. I lived in this city for a time, and eventually I moved to Louisiana."

Then she told him about Mrs. Travilla's estate at Viamede. She made a point of saying that she had been a housekeeper, and she saw with approval that he didn't so much as blink at the revelation that she had labored with her hands. Talk of Viamede led to a discussion of the Travilla family and the Dinsmores and how Zoe came to live with them.

"You did not choose to stay in Rome, Miss Love?" Monsieur Alphonse asked. Then he added in an offhanded way, "I can understand, for it is a very expensive city."

"Oh, but I could have stayed," Zoe responded. "Papa made sure I was provided for. I could have lived there comfortably

on my inheritance. But Papa wished for me to come to the United States, and the Dinsmores and Mrs. Travilla welcomed me like family."

"And now you live on a plantation," he said. "Is it very large and very beautiful?"

"Ever so beautiful," Zoe said. "The Oaks and Ion are huge places, though they call them farms now—not plantations. I think I could walk for miles and miles and not come to the end of them."

"There is great wealth in land here," Monsieur Alphonse noted. "I have observed how American men who make their fortunes in industry soon buy land for themselves. They move to the country and build houses like castles for their families and live like kings. In Europe, few people can afford castles anymore. They are much too hard to heat," he added with a laugh. "But I was led to believe that most Southerners lost their wealth in the Civil War."

"I think the Dinsmores and the Travillas suffered some losses, but they are excellent business people," Zoe explained. "Mrs. Travilla is amazingly clever. She manages all of her properties and businesses just as if she were a man. And she's incredibly generous to others."

Mrs. O'Flaherty was listening with interest when she realized that this talk of money and property was not appropriate for her and Zoe. So she quickly changed the subject by asking the monsieur if he had attended the theater while in the city. He had seen several performances and regaled the ladies with delightful stories about a number of famous actors and actresses whom he knew.

Then he made a suggestion. "This has been such a pleasant visit, but I am sorry that Miss Travilla was not here. Perhaps you ladies would allow me to return your hospitality. I should like to take you both and Miss Travilla to dinner and the theater if you have no other plans on Saturday. You would be doing me a great favor. My hosts, the Despards, will be out of town for the weekend, so I will be on my own. A night at the theater is always more enjoyable when shared with good companions."

Zoe was almost bouncing with excitement, but Mrs. O'Flaherty said in an unusually formal way, "It is a gracious invitation, Monsieur, but we must consult with Miss Travilla. I'm sure you understand. We will speak to her when she returns, and she will communicate with you."

"I completely understand," he said with a charming smile. "I hope you will encourage her to accept. She can write to me at the Despards'. And now, I must take my leave."

He bowed and said, "Thank you so much for sharing your tea and your company with a wandering stranger."

When he had gone, Zoe broke into a happy little dance. "A night at the theater!" she exclaimed. "I hope, I hope Vi will agree! Do you think she will, Mrs. O? And what did you think of Monsieur Alphonse?"

"I think he is both gracious and interesting," Mrs. O'Flaherty replied. "But we know very little about him. Vi may choose to decline, and you must not be disappointed."

"I will be disappointed," Zoe said, "but I promise not to show it."

"That will have to do," Mrs. O'Flaherty said with an understanding smile.

In the lobby of the hotel, Monsieur Alphonse was met by a short, round man dressed all in brown.

"Was it a productive visit, sir?" the man asked.

"Very," the monsieur replied. "I learned much that I needed to know. She is quite remarkable, Biggs, quite a remarkable person."

"Then you will proceed with your plan?" Mr. Biggs asked.

"For certain," the Frenchman replied with a knowing smile. "I think it will be a most profitable venture. Come now. It is time to set things in motion."

When Vi returned, Zoe told her of Monsieur Alphonse's visit and his invitation. Zoe was not disappointed, for Vi agreed to accept and wrote a note to the gentleman for delivery the next morning.

Later that night, after Zoe had gone to bed, Vi and Mrs. O'Flaherty took time for a chat.

"I think our Zoe may have a little crush on Monsieur Alphonse," Vi smiled.

"She is at that age," Mrs. O'Flaherty replied. "And the gentleman is very attentive to her."

"How do you mean?" Vi asked.

Mrs. O'Flaherty said, "Oh, he's quite correct in his behavior. He speaks to her as a good uncle might. He asks questions and listens to her with interest. I am sure his attention is flattering to Zoe. We must remember that she is more used to the company of adults than of people her own age."

Vi thought she heard a slight hesitation in Mrs. O'Flaherty's response. So she asked, "And what did *you* think of him, Mrs. O?"

Violet's Turning Point

Pondering for a few moments, Mrs. O'Flaherty at last replied, "He was perhaps too inquisitive about your family and the Dinsmores. But then I may be overly sensitive. His questions were natural enough, I suppose. On the other hand, he learned much about us yet told us almost nothing about himself."

"Do you mistrust his motives?" Vi asked with concern.

"I have no reason to," Mrs. O'Flaherty said. "I'm sure I'm just being excessively cautious. I will never forget Zoe's grief when her father died. I saw then how vulnerable she is. She is so lively and self-confident, but beneath the surface, she is still a young girl who just recently lost the most important person in her life."

Vi nodded in agreement. "She is complicated, isn't she? Sophisticated but not at all worldly. Zoe often astonishes me with the wisdom of her observations. She sometimes seems years ahead of me in her understanding of people. But all the same, I want to wrap my arms around her and protect her from anyone and anything that could hurt her."

"It is always difficult to know how much we should protect others—especially young people," Mrs. O'Flaherty mused. "Perhaps we should take our lesson from the birds. They understand that their fledglings must be released from the nest if they are to learn to fly."

"My Papa used to say that," Vi replied in a soft tone. "He said that if a person was to soar, he had to learn to fly first. He said it was hard for parents to let go, but it was an act of love."

Vi's words reminded Mrs. O'Flaherty of a decision that had to be made. "Speaking of letting go," she said, "Zoe has asked if she might venture out alone on occasion. Just short walks to the nearby shops. She was used to such freedom in Rome, and I think she misses her independence."

A Surprise Visitor

"That would be all right, I suppose," Vi said. "Not at night, of course."

"She asked only to take walks about this neighborhood and the park in the afternoon."

"As long as she tells you exactly where she is going and returns at the agreed time," Vi said. Then she laughed, "Listen to me, Mrs. O. I sound exactly like an anxious parent!"

"There's no harm in that, Vi girl," Mrs. O'Flaherty said. "Someday you'll be a parent and face such decisions day in and day out. In this case, you've made the right decision, and it will make our little fledgling very happy indeed."

Before going to bed, Vi wrote to her brother. She wanted Ed to know how well things were going. She wrote about her experiences at Dr. Frazier's clinic—how she planned to go there every chance she had before the end of the trip and how much she was learning from the doctor. She wrote about the visits with the Despards and their other social engagements. In passing, she mentioned the French art dealer who had been so kind to invite her and Zoe and Mrs. O'Flaherty to the theater and how much they all looked forward to their evening as the guests of Monsieur Francois Alphonse. She also updated him on the amazing recovery of Virginia and the baby and Louise's extraordinary change of heart. Bringing her letter to its close, Vi wrote:

Our visit here is like a strange journey of discovery for me. I spend my days at the clinic where I am with people who have so little that even a slice of bread or a cup of milk is a treasure. Then I come back to this beautiful hotel where I need only ask for something and it is delivered. I visit the homes of people whose wealth enables them to have every material thing a person could want and gives them the time to indulge their love of art and books and music. It is as if I were traveling back and forth between two distant planets, yet the people I meet on each planet are not as different as they may believe.

For a long time, I've thought that I was called to help the poor. But the people at the clinic are helping me! Each day I see more clearly their courage in the face of such terrible obstacles. Not all the people there are believers, but most have the kind of faith that can move mountains. Even in the bleakest of circumstances, their hope does not dim. Still, the gap between those who have and those who don't seems almost too wide to bridge. But we know that we are all one! Paul explained it so clearly in 1 Corinthians: "The body is a unit, though it is made up of many parts; and though all its parts are many, they form one body. So it is with Christ. For we are all baptized by one Spirit into one body—whether Jews or Greeks, slave or free—and we were all given the one Spirit to drink." More than ever, Ed, I'm seeing here how necessary we all are to one another.

Dr. Frazier says that the Lord is giving me this opportunity to test my commitment and see my path more clearly. Mother intended this trip to be a holiday for Zoe and me, and it is. But I know that God intended something more. It was His plan that we find Virginia and little Betsy. It was His plan that we meet

Dr. Frazier. In His infinite wisdom, He brings us to turning points, and we make choices. I feel in some way that I am near a turning point, that the time has come for me to choose the direction my life will take. Pray for me, Ed, because I really want to see God's plan for my life and follow His path. When I see you next, I hope we'll have time for some good, long chats, like we always had when you were living at home. As I look into my future, it's so comforting to know that I have you and Mamma to help me make the right choices.

CHAPTER

11

Busy Days
and Nights

*Perfume and incense bring joy to
the heart, and the pleasantness
of one's friend springs from
his earnest counsel.*

PROVERBS 27:9

*T*he next five days seemed to fly by. Vi spent at least part of every day at the clinic, doing whatever Dr. Frazier needed. Several nights she joined the doctor for dinner. Their conversations revolved primarily around the work of the clinic and the practical aspects of a medical ministry. But they also talked about the doctor's other interests, and Vi learned about the suffrage movement and the work of women across the country to establish services for the poor.

"So you believe that getting the right to vote will enable women to affect the decisions made by the government?" Vi asked one evening as they were enjoying coffee after another of Amelia's plain but filling meals.

"It is a first step," Amelia said. "I believe that women have much to bring to offer. Of course, wives have always been able to influence their husbands and mothers their sons—more or less. But until now, women haven't had the chance to raise their own voices in the public arena. Getting the right to vote would bring recognition that we are all citizens of this great nation, male and female alike."

"But would that make a difference?" Vi wondered.

"I truly think it would," Amelia replied. "As wives and mothers, daughters and sisters, we women often have a different perspective from our husbands and fathers and brothers and sons. If women participate in decision making, I believe we can create a more balanced approach to the problems we all face. Child labor, for instance, is a disgrace. Children like Michael, the boy who was so terribly injured at the laundry, must be protected. They must be allowed to have their childhood and be given every opportunity to grow strong and learn. If more women understood what life is like for a child in a city tenement, I believe they would demand change."

Amelia spoke of such things with a passion that never failed to inspire Vi. The doctor also told Vi about her own childhood and youth and the difficulties she faced when she determined to become a physician.

"There are a great many myths about women," Amelia said with a half-smile, "and you will have to do battle with all of them. The worst is that we are weaker in mind than men and so education is wasted on us."

"Do people really think that?" Vi asked. "In my family, no one has ever suggested that I or my sisters are any less capable of learning than my brothers are."

"You are most fortunate," Amelia responded with a sigh. "My father, who was the dearest man, could not understand my wish to become a doctor. He thought it was just a whim that would fade away as soon as I found myself a good husband. It was my mother who encouraged me—and Marguerite, too—to make the most of our minds and our talents. My father never admitted that he approved of my profession, but he loved and respected my mother, so he finally gave in."

Amelia paused for a few moments and smiled to herself. Then she said, "In the end, he was secretly proud of my choices. He wouldn't say so to me. But he talked to my mother, and she told me what he said—just as he knew she would. He didn't live to see this clinic, and I wonder what he would have thought of it. I imagine he would have chided me about wasting my money and not going to parties to meet eligible bachelors. Then I expect he'd have written a large check for my work."

Amelia quoted from the nineteenth chapter of Matthew: " 'Again I tell you, it is easier for a camel to go through the eye of a needle than for a rich man to enter the kingdom of God.' "

Vi's eyes widened. "I was reading that very story last night!" she exclaimed. "Reminding myself what Jesus told the rich young man to do. I worry that I cannot give up everything I have to serve others. When we were in Rome last summer, I saw something of what it is like to be poor in a huge city. But here at the clinic and in this neighborhood, I've learned much more about the lives of people who have so very little. I wrote something to my brother recently. I told him how, here in New York, I feel as if I were living on two planets, traveling back and forth between the lovely world of teas and dinner parties and beautiful people, and the world of poverty and illness and injustice. And I must choose one world or the other. I'm not sure I can make that choice."

Amelia leaned forward and said, "Remember what Jesus said to the rich young man: 'To be perfect, go, sell your possessions and give to the poor, and you will have treasure in heaven. Then come, follow me.'

"I studied that story very hard when I was deciding to return from Paris and start the clinic," the doctor went on. "Frankly, it was my parents' wealth that enabled me to become a physician and study abroad. I knew in my heart that I was following God's path, but if I gave up all my wealth, how then could I serve the poor? Without money, how could I run this clinic? It seemed a great dilemma until I realized what Jesus was really telling us. In directing the young man to sell his possessions, I believe our Lord was saying that having wealth is a responsibility, not a gift for the mere pleasure of the wealthy. The young man had a choice to make—to follow the Lord or to cling to his possessions. Jesus was talking about the depth of the man's faith, not the size of his bank account. Would the young man be willing to sacrifice the treasures of this world to achieve the eternal treasures of the next?"

Vi said, "I've read the passage so many times, and it seems to me that Jesus had great compassion for the young man. I've often wondered why the rich man went away. Was he just too greedy?"

Amelia thought for a moment. "That's possible, but somehow I don't think so," she said. "We know that he went away in sadness. I think perhaps his trouble was that he *defined* himself by his money. I've known very many people like that. They don't love wealth for its own sake but for its benefits here on this earth—things like social position and special privileges and the kind of respect that rich people get merely because they're rich. They don't understand that they need not literally give everything away, but that God wants them to give up their *attachment* to their worldly goods, for money and material objects offer no hope of eternal salvation. Such people suffer from a poverty of the soul, because they cannot imagine a life beyond their possessions. Perhaps the young man was afraid of how he would be treated if he abandoned his earthly treasures. Maybe he thought that having wealth made him special. He forgot that everyone is special to our Lord."

Picking up on Amelia's thought, Vi said, "The young man wanted eternal life, but he wasn't able to look beyond his earthly life. He was stuck where he was, like an animal mired in a swamp, and he couldn't see his way to follow God's path. He wasn't willing to open his heart all the way to the Lord."

"But in the story, Jesus does not rebuke him," Amelia noted. "Jesus looked into the young man's heart and knew how difficult the struggle was. Jesus didn't just tell the young man to give away his material wealth. He offered the young man a new path—a new purpose in life. The Bible doesn't tell us what the man eventually did, but if he chose redemption and eternal life, we can be sure that Jesus would be there for him, showing him the way."

"So it is the *purpose* that wealth is used for that is the difficulty," Vi mused.

Amelia smiled again and said, "I don't think that you must choose between those two planets you spoke of, Vi. Remember what Paul wrote to Timothy, that 'the *love* of money is a root of all kinds of evil.' You don't love money, my friend. You love the Lord, and you want to follow Him by serving others. You have already made the most important choice by choosing to live your faith as He directs you to. I don't believe that there is a commandment against enjoying ourselves occasionally," the doctor added wryly. "If I had not accepted Marguerite's invitation to dine at Domenici's that night, you and I might never have become friends."

"That's so true," Vi agreed. "But still, I can't help feeling guilty somehow, knowing the kind of suffering that so many people endure every day. My eyes have been opened to the real meaning of poverty, yet I don't suffer."

Amelia waved her hand in a dismissive way and said, "Guilty feelings won't achieve anything, Vi. As a physician, I must deal with my failures all the time. When that boy,

Michael, was brought in here, I did everything I could to save his arm, yet I could not, nor could the surgeons. I felt frustrated that my profession is not yet so advanced that we have the knowledge to repair such grievous injuries. I felt anger at the terrible working conditions that cause such accidents. But I didn't feel guilt, because I knew that I had done my best for that child. Every day, I must sort through those things I can control and those that are out of my hands. If I feel guilty about everything I cannot control, I won't be much of a doctor, for misplaced guilt makes us timid and fearful."

Amelia stopped for a moment to take a sip of her coffee. Then she said, "God has blessed you and your family with material abundance, and He has His reasons. That is where you must begin—trusting His purpose. It isn't what you have that matters. It's what you *do* with what you have. Feeling guilty because you have more than others does nothing to help them. There are times when we should feel guilty, of course, as when we break our Lord's commandment to love one another. To use one's wealth to harm or deceive— that is a cause for guilt. But to feel guilty just because you've been given advantages is to doubt His purpose, isn't it? God has given you the capacity to find joy in this life and in the promise of eternal life with Him. Isn't that what you want to share with others? Isn't your family's wealth, which will be yours someday, one more tool to achieve God's purpose and share the joy of knowing Him?"

When Vi left the clinic that night, her friend's questions rang in her mind. Amelia had opened a new level of understanding to her. Vi had always trusted God to lead her to the right path. But now she saw that she was already on that path—that she had been on it since her birth. As if a bright lamp had been turned on, the full extent of the blessings she'd been given was illuminated: Her parents and her family and their teachings. The education she'd received not only from books but also from opportunities to travel and see how other people lived. The chance to experience the joys as well as the sorrows of life. The path of her life had been leading her to this point.

Her prayer that night was filled with excitement. *Yes, oh yes! I trust Your purpose, dear Father in Heaven! I know I will make mistakes, maybe big mistakes. But You have given me the means to do what's right and follow the path You have set for me. I understand now! Each person's path is different, and each of us must find our own way. You light the way for us, but it's up to us to follow Your light. Oh, how glorious Your plan is, dear Father! Every life follows a different course, and I can't presume to know what is best for others. Feeling guilty because my life seems easier than others is like taking a wrong turn because it makes me fearful and leads me away from Your purpose for me. Thank You, God, for helping me to see more clearly what trust in Your limitless love and wisdom really means.*

Energized with the new thoughts and prayers sparked by her recent talk with Dr. Frazier, Vi no longer felt torn between the two worlds she was experiencing in New York. The exhilaration she felt at the clinic, watching and learning from Dr. Frazier, was in no way diminished by the pleasure of a night at the opera with Mr. and Mrs. Phillips or afternoon tea with Mrs. Vangelt. In fact, by week's end, Vi was almost as excited as Zoe by the prospect of Monsieur Alphonse's invitation to dinner and the theater.

Violet's Turning Point

Whatever doubts Vi may have had about the charming Frenchman were put soon away. The monsieur was as considerate a host as any of them had ever known. The play he chose was a light comedy and, as Mrs. O'Flaherty remarked to Vi, entirely suitable for a girl of Zoe's age.

At dinner, they learned a bit more about Monsieur Alphonse. He said that he had studied to be a painter, but alas, he did not have the talent to be great. So he had become a dealer in art and a student of art history. At some point in the conversation, Zoe asked if he had ever seen the work of an artist named Lester Leland.

"But of course!" Monsieur Alphonse replied. "He is the young American who lives in Rome. He is not so well known yet, but I saw a number of his portraits at a small gallery in Paris. He has a unique style, I think, and I believe that he will make a great success. But how do you know him?"

Vi explained that Lester was married to her sister.

"Is your sister a beautiful young woman with golden brown hair and hazel eyes?" he asked.

When Vi said that she was, Monsieur Alphonse clapped his hands in glee. "Then I have seen her portrait!" he exclaimed. "It was on display in the gallery, but it was not for sale. The gallery owner told me most emphatically that Mr. Leland would not part with the painting for any amount of money. Now that I know she is his wife, I can understand."

There was only one jarring note in the otherwise perfect evening. As they were entering the restaurant, Vi thought she saw the silent Mr. Biggs standing behind a column in the entrance foyer. She just caught a glimpse before the man disappeared. Curious, she asked Monsieur Alphonse if his business associate would be joining them for dinner.

"He is not so comfortable at social gatherings," Monsieur Alphonse replied. "As you doubtless observed that after-noon at the Despards', Mr. Biggs does not have what you call a 'knack' for conversation."

Vi naturally assumed that she had been in error. She had only seen someone who resembled Mr. Biggs. It was not until several days later that she recalled the incident and realized that Monsieur Alphonse had not answered her question.

CHAPTER

A Cause for Worry?

*Do not be anxious about anything,
but in everything, by prayer and
petition, with thanksgiving,
present your requests
to God.*

PHILIPPIANS 4:6

A Cause for Worry?

*C*al and Arthur Conley arrived the following Tuesday. Arthur examined his sister and her baby, and he pronounced them both fit for travel. Vi hoped her cousins might stay for a few days and see the city, but their visit was only to be overnight. They were all anxious to return to Roselands.

The next morning, as the others were finishing their packing, Louise came to Vi's room.

"I want to thank you again, my dear, for all that you have done," Louise began. "You are a brave young woman, and a tolerant one. I regret that I never made much effort to know you and your brothers and sisters as you were growing up."

Vi started to say something, but Louise took her hand and continued, "I have much to make amends for. I know that not everyone will forgive me. But I will do my best to earn forgiveness, and I know our Lord will help me."

"You were very brave too, Aunt Louise," Vi said gently. "If you hadn't been so determined to find Virginia—"

Louise interrupted, "I can't bear to think how often I wanted to turn back that day. But you pressed on, Vi. You trusted your heart, and because of that I have Virginia and little Betsy now. I have a second chance. I will give my granddaughter what I failed to give my own children—the knowledge of God's love for all His children."

"There is no greater gift," Vi said, her voice choking.

Her aunt took her into a warm embrace. "Thank you, Vi," Louise whispered, "and I will never forget your kindness to me when I did not deserve it."

"I love you, Aunt Louise," Vi said. "I really do."

Violet's Turning Point

She hugged Vi even tighter. After some moments Louise stood back. "We both need to wipe our eyes," she said as she pulled a lace handkerchief from her sleeve. "One of the first things I will do when I get home is to see your mother. I want her to know what you have done and how much you mean to me—to all of us."

"Just tell her that we're fine and that we are looking forward to our homecoming," Vi said. "Just tell her how much I love her and miss her."

"I will tell her, dear child, and a great deal more."

Louise wiped the tears from her eyes and made a little show of brushing at her skirt. "I really should dress in brighter colors," she said. "I have so much to be joyful for. Perhaps when you return to Ion, Mrs. O'Flaherty might help me with some shopping. She is such a good companion. I see why you girls love her so. I see so many things now that I never saw before."

There was a knock at the door, and Louise's eldest son, Cal Conley, came in.

"We must go now, Mother," he said, "or we will miss our train."

Louise put out her arms to Vi once more and kissed her cheek. Then she left.

But Cal lingered for a minute.

"Thank you, Vi," he said. "I am not always as observant as I should be. But it has dawned on me at last that my cousin has become a remarkable young lady. I hope you know what you have helped to accomplish. I believe that my family will be healed now."

"I have faith that it will," Vi said with a radiant smile. Then her expression became serious, and she asked, "Have you any plans to search for Mr. Neuville?"

A Cause for Worry?

Cal's brow furrowed. "Arthur and I have talked about it," he replied. "But we have decided not to pursue him. In truth, Vi, I am almost afraid of what I might do if I caught up with the scoundrel. There might be some reason to seek him in the future. He is little Betsy's father after all. But I hope we never have to. I hope Virginia never has to be reminded of him again."

"But she won't forget all that she's been through," Vi said.

"No, she won't forget," he mused, "but she needs to forgive herself."

"She and Aunt Louise have made a good start," Vi smiled. "They have found God again, as your mother likes to say. He will help Virginia. She was very courageous, you know. She was ready to sacrifice herself for her child."

Cal smiled again. "That baby is a blessing for us all, Vi. Now don't you worry. We're all together now, as a family and in faith. Will you come down to see us off?"

"It would be my pleasure," Vi said. She looped her arm through his, and they left the suite. As they walked down the stairs, Cal told her what was happening back in the South. Her mother and brothers and sister were all well. The big news was that Vi's little brother, Danny, was taking jumping lessons on his pony.

"You should see him, Vi," Cal was saying when they reached the hotel lobby. "When he takes those low jumps, Danny looks like a miniature of your father."

"You're making me homesick," Vi sighed.

"We all miss you," her cousin said. He kissed her lightly on the top of her head and walked to the hotel doors. "Come and wave us good-bye!" he called back to her.

She followed him outside and watched as he climbed into the waiting carriage with his mother, brother, sister, and sweet little Betsy. Vi waved mightily as the carriage moved into the busy street, and she kept waving until she could no longer see them.

~———~

The three women were in the sitting room of their suite. Vi was trying to read a book, but she kept thinking about her family and summer back at Ion, and couldn't focus on the page. Mrs. O'Flaherty was mending a petticoat hem, but after a few stitches she paused with her needle in midair, and a faraway expression came into her eyes. Zoe was flipping aimlessly through a magazine.

"I really miss your Aunt Louise," Zoe said suddenly. "And Virginia and Betsy."

Vi put her book aside and said, "I've been thinking about home."

"As have I," Mrs. O'Flaherty agreed. "But we cannot let ourselves mope, girls. We have ten more days in New York, and much more to see and do."

Zoe sat forward and clasped her hands together. "We've been invited to the Despards' this afternoon. All of us. Do you think you might go, Vi? It's always so cheerful there."

"Well, I told Dr. Frazier that I couldn't come to the clinic today because of family matters," Vi said.

"Oh, good, you can go!" Zoe exclaimed. "I know Mrs. Despard will be glad. She always asks about you, and I've told her about your going to the clinic to help her sister. Mrs. Despard says that she doesn't understand why her sister works so hard, but she really admires what she's doing for others. They are very different, aren't they? I used to think that sisters would be alike."

A Cause for Worry?

"That's what makes families so interesting, Zoe," said Mrs. O'Flaherty. "The people in them are individuals and therefore unpredictable. Now come, and we can select a dress for you to wear this afternoon. Mr. Meriweather will be here for us at three o'clock."

The gathering at Marguerite Despard's was not nearly so formal as the first time Vi visited. There were five young women present, and all were around Mrs. Despard's age. The conversation was almost girlish, Vi thought, and she joined in delightedly.

Mr. Despard arrived at four o'clock, followed shortly after by Monsieur Alphonse, with Mr. Biggs just behind him. Vi had a sudden image of Mr. Biggs as a fat, brown hound at his master's heels.

Vi lost track of Mr. Biggs as three more gentlemen came in. They were the husbands of three of the ladies. It was a very convivial crowd, and there was much laughter in the parlor. Vi was talking to the two single ladies when Marguerite Despard joined them. They all chatted for a time, until Mrs. Despard said, "Vi, I have something I'd like to show you in the library."

With a polite excuse to her other guests, Mrs. Despard took Vi's arm and led her to a handsome, wood-paneled room opposite the parlor. Vi looked around at the wall of bookcases filled with leather-covered volumes. Then she saw a painting on an easel, and she assumed this was what Mrs. Despard wanted her to see. She didn't notice that Mrs. Despard had closed the library door.

"It's a wonderful room," Vi said.

"Yes, it is," Mrs. Despard replied almost absentmindedly. "But in truth, I have nothing to show you. I wanted a few minutes of privacy. There is something I need to discuss with you. It may be a problem."

At Vi's quizzical expression, Mrs. Despard went on, "Our houseguest, Monsieur Alphonse, has taken an interest in young Zoe. I had no concerns, for it seemed natural that, given Zoe's background in Europe, they would have much in common. I honestly thought that Francois regarded Zoe as he might a younger sister. But when Zoe came to tea last week, I overheard a conversation that has worried me greatly. I don't make it a practice to eavesdrop, but I was looking for Francois, and I came to this room. The door was partly open, and I heard his and Zoe's voices. I was about to enter, but what I heard stopped me."

Vi's expression had become very serious. "What did you hear, Mrs. Despard?" she asked.

"Mind you, I only heard part of the conversation. It may have been completely innocent," Mrs. Despard said. It was clear that she was upset, and she hesitated for a few seconds. Then she took a deep breath and continued.

"Francois was saying, 'I believe we can do it without anyone knowing. I have made all the arrangements.' And then Zoe said how clever he was and that she could keep the secret. At that, Francois warned her that it was especially important that neither you nor Mrs. O'Flaherty should suspect anything. He said that it would take a few more days and that everyone would be happy when they found out. At that point I rapped on the door and walked in. They both looked very surprised, but I acted normally. I can be a rather good actress, so I don't think they realized that I was listening. Oh, I hope they didn't!"

She began to twist her slender fingers and added, "I didn't know whether to tell you, but I worried all weekend

while we were away in the country. Francois is staying with us at the recommendation of an old friend in Washington. But beyond that recommendation, Chris and I really know very little about him. Do you think he could be a fortune hunter after Zoe's inheritance? It happens often enough these days. Young women with money are so vulnerable to men with charm and European manners."

Mrs. Despard almost collapsed onto a chair. "But it may be nothing," she said again, as if to assure herself.

"I think it was probably innocent," Vi said, speaking with a confidence she didn't feel. She sat down in the chair next to Mrs. Despard. "What you heard sounds strange, but we don't know the subject of the conversation. Monsieur Alphonse might be arranging a purchase for Zoe. She really loves secrets and surprises. Now that I think about it, he is probably helping her buy something for me and Mrs. O'Flaherty. Or something for my Mamma. It would be just like Zoe to give us gifts to thank us for this trip."

"Do you really think that?" Mrs. Despard asked hopefully. "If that's true, I will feel properly embarrassed for jumping to conclusions. I *want* to be wrong. I want very much to be wrong."

"But you are right—and very kind—to be so concerned," Vi said gently. "Zoe is young and enthusiastic. Girls her age are vulnerable to flattery. But she is also very level-headed. There is a great deal of common sense in her—more than most people appreciate."

"Will you say anything to her?" Mrs. Despard asked.

Vi considered. She said, "No, but I will speak to Mrs. O'Flaherty. Zoe has given us no reason to distrust her, but we can be watchful."

Violet's Turning Point

Mrs. Despard straightened her shoulders and set her mouth in a determined little smile. "And I shall be watchful of Francois," she said. "I have told no one else of this—not even Chris. And I shan't say a word unless you ask me to."

"Let's keep it to ourselves for now," Vi said.

"I'm so glad you came today," Mrs. Despard said, laying her hand on Vi's arm. "I have a very active imagination, and I'm sure that I have just given in to it. But Chris and I have come to regard you and Zoe as real friends—just like Ed. I couldn't let anyone hurt any of you."

"And Monsieur Alphonse?" Vi questioned. "I hope this won't color your opinion of him."

"I won't let it," Mrs. Despard said firmly. "He should not be the victim of my imagination. Still, I shall be relieved when he returns to France."

Leaning close to Vi, she confided, "His visit has been very stressful. Every woman I know wants to meet him and sit beside him at dinner. Since he arrived, I seem to have done nothing but hold teas and dinner parties. And still I can't please all the eager ladies."

"There's no denying that Monsieur Alphonse is very attractive," Vi replied as they went arm-in-arm back to the parlor and the guests. She spotted the monsieur on the other side of the room. He was talking with the two single ladies, and Vi saw they were enraptured by whatever he was saying.

Very attractive, she thought, *but what is he really? Why does he tell so little about himself? And how can I find out what is true and what is false?*

158

A Cause for Worry?

Vi was somewhat subdued at supper that evening, but Zoe was so excited about the people she had met at the Despards' that she didn't notice. Mrs. O'Flaherty, however, did observe the change in Vi's mood. At bedtime, she came to Vi's room and asked if she was feeling all right.

"Just a little tired," Vi said.

Mrs. O'Flaherty sat down on the side of Vi's bed and said, "Working with Dr. Frazier does not seem to fatigue you."

Vi said softly, "Perhaps that's because helping at the clinic has purpose. Parties are more tiring, but Dr. Frazier is helping me overcome my guilty feelings about enjoying social pleasures."

With a smile, Mrs. O'Flaherty said, "You may not think it, but no matter how important the work you do, you need breaks now and then. Remember the lesson of Ecclesiastes: 'There is a time for everything, and a season for every activity under heaven.' The teacher tells how he learns to love all of God's gifts. 'I know that there is nothing better for men than to be happy and do good while they live. That everyone may eat and drink, and find satisfaction in all his toil — this is the gift of God.' "

Mrs. O'Flaherty put a strong arm around Vi's shoulder and went on. "When my husband was alive, he used to say that allowing ourselves time for simple pleasures made our toil meaningful. Some of my fondest memories are of evenings when Ian would play for our friends. He worked so hard on his compositions, but there were occasions when friends would gather in our small apartment, and we would dine on cheese and bread and fruit. Then he would play pieces that he'd written — play just for the sheer love of the music. He would forget the toil and stress for a time, and when he returned to his work the next day, it was always with renewed energy and determination."

Vi imagined what such gatherings must have been like — the music and the warmth of supportive friends. "Do you miss those times very much?" she asked.

"Not exactly," Mrs. O'Flaherty replied. "I miss Ian and always will. But I have my memories, and they are very sweet. His music is as alive for me today as it was when he wrote it—though I haven't heard it played in many years."

"I'd like to hear it," Vi said.

"Perhaps you shall, someday," Mrs. O'Flaherty said. "There is a time for everything." Her words seemed to trail away, like ripples in the water trailing after a boat.

Vi looked into Mrs. O'Flaherty's face and saw a mix of sadness and strength that tugged at her heart. But Mrs. O'Flaherty, who was not often given to expressions of sentimentality, quickly rearranged her expression into its usual look.

"Well, now," she said, patting Vi's shoulder. "It's settled. You need not feel guilty about having a good time at Mrs. Despard's parties. We might both take a lesson from Zoe, for I have never known a girl who had more fun in the company of others."

"Do you think . . ." Vi began. Then she paused, deciding exactly how to phrase her question before asking, "Do you think that all this activity might be too—ah—too stimulating for her? I worry that she may find life at home very dull when we return."

"Zoe is one of those people who does not allow life to be dull," Mrs. O'Flaherty answered with a chuckle.

"Still, I think we should be watchful of her," Vi said.

"Has she done something that troubles you?" Mrs. O'Flaherty asked with a note of concern.

"No, not at all," Vi replied quickly. "I just remembered what you said before we got to New York. You said she was at an age when common sense could be overcome by curiosity and a spirit of adventure. I haven't spent as much time with Zoe as I should, and I feel responsible for her."

Mrs. O'Flaherty knew very well how strong Vi's sense of responsibility was. So she responded seriously. "I will be watchful, but I don't think you need to worry. Zoe is enjoying her visit here immensely. But she told me just yesterday that she is looking forward to being at Ion and The Oaks again. She feels a little homesick, and that's a good sign."

"Why?" Vi asked. "I don't usually think of homesickness as a good thing."

"But in this instance," Mrs. O'Flaherty said, "it means that she is homesick for your family. And that tells me she feels that your family is also *her* family. Her new family—where she is loved. That is a very positive step for a young girl who was so recently orphaned."

"I see," Vi said thoughtfully, and she felt better.

~

Mrs. O'Flaherty's observation had encouraged Vi, so she didn't tell her about the conversation that Mrs. Despard had overheard. *No need to worry Mrs. O when there is probably nothing to worry about. Probably? Why can't I shake this anxiety?* Vi thought as she lay in the dark and tried to get to sleep. *Maybe I'm feeling a little guilty about not being as attentive to Zoe as I should. But that conversation between Zoe and Monsieur Alphonse—what was it really about? And how lonely does Zoe really feel?*

Vi turned over and squeezed her eyes shut. But she could not escape her thoughts. *I've promised to go to the clinic tomorrow, but after that I will make more time for Zoe. Still—that conversation. Could Mrs. Despard be right? Could Monsieur Alphonse be a fortune hunter? Could Zoe be the innocent victim of an evil scheme? How can I discover the truth? I could confront Zoe—but what if I'm wrong? She would never trust me again. What can I do? Dear Lord, help me to find the answer!*

She tossed restlessly and she could almost hear the minutes ticking by. Her mind boiled with ideas. *We could go home early, but what excuse could I give? I could write to Mamma for advice, but how can I burden her when there is probably no problem at all?*

Probably—that word again! I have to do something. Suddenly, she had the answer to her prayer. *Ed will help! I must write to him and tell him everything. I promised that I would let him know if I needed help, and now I am in need.*

She sat up and said into the darkness, "Thank You, dear Father in Heaven, for Your love and Your guidance never fail us! 'Your word is a lamp to my feet and a light for my path.' "

Then she lay down again, and at last she slept.

CHAPTER

Deepening Suspicions

*The end of a matter is better
than its beginning, and
patience is better
than pride.*

ECCLESIASTES 7:8

Deepening Suspicions

_V_i was up at dawn, and she penned her letter to Ed as the sun rose over the park. She looked up from her writing to see how the sunlight seemed to dart in and out among the trees, sweeping up the shadows of night and restoring the color to everything. _It's going to be a sunny summer day,_ she thought, and she finished her letter with a lighter heart.

Mrs. O'Flaherty had planned a full day of sightseeing with Zoe, beginning with a visit to the Museum of Natural History. Then Vi and Zoe would have dinner with Mr. and Mrs. Phillips that night. After posting her letter to Ed, Vi left for the clinic knowing that Zoe would be fully occupied; there would be no tea parties and no chances for encounters with Monsieur Alphonse.

Vi worked all day with Dr. Frazier, and when she left the clinic at three o'clock, she felt happy and invigorated. She almost regretted sending her letter to Ed. She was becoming convinced that she had over-reacted to Mrs. Despard's story. _Ed said that we are a henhouse,_ she thought. _And here I am clucking about Zoe just like an old mother hen!_ It felt good to laugh at herself. In fact, she felt so good that she asked Mr. Meriweather to stop the carriage on the side of the park opposite the hotel. She wanted to walk through the park and savor the beauty of the afternoon.

Central Park was full of people strolling and children playing. Handsome open carriages drove back and forth on its wide avenues, as their passengers enjoyed the fine summer afternoon. There was a leisurely atmosphere that reflected Vi's own feelings. She wandered down a flower-bordered path that meandered among the trees and lawns and finally took her out of the park and onto the avenue. She realized that she was at least two blocks away from the hotel. She looked around to get her bearings, and her gaze fell on a sight that made her heart sink.

Zoe was just coming out of an office building on the other side of the street. And Monsieur Alphonse was holding the door for her!

Vi couldn't think. She felt glued to the sidewalk, unable to move or turn away. But neither Zoe nor Monsieur Alphonse looked in her direction. They were standing close together, and Zoe was talking and gesturing excitedly. Suddenly, she grasped Monsieur Alphonse's hand and pressed it to her lips. Then the monsieur leaned forward and gently caressed Zoe's cheek with his hand.

It was over in seconds. Zoe opened her parasol and turned in the direction of the hotel. She walked away as if she were dancing on clouds. When Vi looked back at the entrance to the building, she saw Monsieur Alphonse going in the opposite direction.

Vi's mind seemed blank. But then a thought hit her like a storm: *It's true! And Zoe is in terrible danger!*

The realization seemed to revive her strength, and she also turned toward the hotel. She didn't try to overtake Zoe. First, she needed to find Mrs. O'Flaherty.

As she walked, Vi kept thinking over and over how she had failed Zoe. There must have been signs that she had missed. Had she been so preoccupied with her own interests that she had been blind to what was obvious? *This is my fault*, she chided herself, *but what matters now is Zoe. Her safety is my responsibility. She doesn't understand how this will ruin her life. She's too young to understand. But I do, and I have to save her from a dreadful mistake.*

As she hurried along, she wasn't aware of the looks of passersby. But several people noticed her and wondered at the expression of the tall, lovely young woman whose dark eyes were so full of trouble.

Vi reached the hotel lobby and was going to the stairway, when the manager stopped her. A letter had come, he said, and he thought it might be important.

He held out an envelope, and Vi took it without looking at it. Thanking him with uncharacteristic curtness, she rushed away. The manager shook his head in bewilderment. He couldn't guess what the problem was, but he very much hoped that Miss Travilla was not dissatisfied with the hotel's service.

The door to Zoe's bedroom was closed, and when Vi walked softly over to it, she heard her little friend singing a tune.

Vi went straight to Mrs. O'Flaherty's room and walked in, forgetting to knock.

Mrs. O'Flaherty looked up and instantly saw the distress in Vi's face.

"What is the matter? What has happened?" she asked, coming to Vi and leading her to a chair. She saw the envelope clutched in Vi's hand and said, "Have you received bad news?"

Vi looked up, and there were tears in her eyes. "I should have told you, Mrs. O," Vi said in a choked voice. "I should have been honest with you."

Mrs. O'Flaherty pulled a stool close, sat down, and took Vi's hand. In a steady but soothing tone, she said, "Well, tell me now, Vi girl. Whatever it is, it will be better when shared."

Violet's Turning Point

It was as if a dam had broken. The whole story poured out in a flood. As she spoke, Vi's tears vanished, and her face flushed with anger.

"What a horrible man!" she exclaimed. "How could I have been so foolish as to trust him?"

Mrs. O'Flaherty was having much the same thought about her own gullibility, but she said, "Now is not the time for blaming ourselves, Vi girl. We must decide what to do."

"I wrote Ed this morning. But I hadn't . . . I hadn't seen—" Vi stammered.

"Well, our first duty is to Zoe," Mrs. O'Flaherty said firmly. "We must not allow her to be anywhere near that man ever again, if it means watching her day and night. There will be no more little walks on her own. One of us must be with her at all times."

"Should we talk to her?" Vi asked.

Mrs. O'Flaherty pondered the question. Finally she said, "You know that my usual impulse is to face every problem directly. In this case, however, confronting Zoe may worsen the situation. If they are planning an elopement, we might push her into it all the faster. But despite everything you've told me, we still do not have absolute proof of her intentions. There may yet be an innocent explanation. I think we'll be able to gauge her feelings better if we do something that I do not like doing."

"What?" Vi asked.

"Ask hinting questions," Mrs. O'Flaherty said flatly. "It's a childish approach, I know, but if we can ask as if we were simply interested in knowing more about Monsieur Alphonse, she may reveal her feelings. Zoe is not a dishonest girl, and I do not believe she could be so bewitched that she would resort to untruths. She won't lie to you, Vi.

She loves and respects you too much. She wouldn't betray you."

"But if she believes that she is in love with that man, she won't betray him either," Vi said.

"That's why we must be sure he is not around to influence her," Mrs. O'Flaherty said. Her confidence in Zoe was raising Vi's spirits again.

"I don't think I am very good at hinting," she said.

"Think about Zoe and her welfare. That will make it easier. Stay calm and behave normally when you talk with her."

"I'll try." Vi took a few deep, slow breaths to steady herself.

There was a light tapping at the door.

"Come in, Zoe," Mrs. O'Flaherty said.

Zoe entered and seeing Vi, she asked, "Are you well? You look feverish."

"She's fine," Mrs. O'Flaherty said. "She's just had a difficult day."

"I'm sorry," Zoe said with genuine concern. "Would you like to cancel our dinner with Mr. and Mrs. Phillips tonight? You've been working so hard at the clinic, Vi. Maybe you need to rest."

Vi smiled and said, "Really, I'm fine. And I want to see Mr. and Mrs. Phillips. I've been thinking what a nice evening it will be."

Mrs. O'Flaherty began to rummage about her dresser. She said to Zoe, "Why don't we select something special for you to wear tonight? I believe several of your new dresses arrived today. I put the boxes in your wardrobe."

Zoe's face lit with a sunny smile. "I'll get them out right now."

"And I'll join you in a few minutes," Mrs. O'Flaherty said.

Violet's Turning Point

Zoe left, and when they heard sounds coming from her room, Vi said in a near whisper, "I really am fine now, Mrs. O, and I'll do my very best to have a pleasant time tonight. Hopefully we can resolve all this very soon. I don't want to do anything that may cause Zoe pain."

"That's the right attitude," Mrs. O'Flaherty said in her most practical way. "Now, you go attend to your dressing, and I'll be in soon to help you button up."

~~~

The evening went very well. Mr. and Mrs. Phillips were especially considerate hosts, and Mr. Phillips devoted much of his time to conversation about the Travillas and the Dinsmores, who had been his friends as well as his clients for many years.

On the ride back from the Phillips' house, Vi dropped Monsieur Alphonse's name several times — as naturally as she could. Zoe answered Vi's questions without hesitation. Vi found herself more confused than ever, for she did not sense that Zoe was withholding anything.

Back at the hotel, the girls chatted for awhile with Mrs. O'Flaherty before getting ready for bed.

"It was nice to hear those stories about your parents and Mr. and Mrs. Dinsmore," Zoe said. "I've had such a wonderful time in New York, but I will really be glad to go home to the South and get back to normal. This would be a big surprise for your grandfather, Vi, but I'm even looking forward to my lessons. Mr. Dinsmore said we will study botany this summer."

Vi cast a quick glance at Mrs. O'Flaherty and then said, "I don't think Grandpapa will be surprised. He says you are a very good student."

"Well, I plan to be much more attentive," Zoe replied. Then she quickly raised her hand to her mouth in the attempt to cover a yawn.

"I saw that," Mrs. O'Flaherty said with a grin. "It's time for all of us to go to our beds."

Zoe stood and said, "I won't argue, Mrs. O."

Zoe and Mrs. O'Flaherty both left, and Vi retired to her own room. She quickly undressed and got into her night-gown. Then she settled into bed and took up her Bible, which Louise had returned to her with much gratitude before leaving for the South. Opening the well-worn book to Lamentations 3, Vi ran her finger down the page and stopped at verses 25–26: "The LORD is good to those whose hope is in him, to the one who seeks him; it is good to wait quietly for the salvation of the LORD."

Vi thought about these verses for some minutes, letting the meaning of the words calm her. "It is good to wait quietly," she said aloud. Then she closed her eyes and prayed, *Lord, I put my hope in You. Keep me from rushing ahead before I am certain of the facts. Give me the strength not to make hasty or false assumptions. I trust You to guide me to the truth.*

Closing her Bible, Vi felt better. She began to think that she had probably been mistaken after all. What she had seen that afternoon was likely only an accidental meeting, and Zoe had been acting as a European girl might. Customs are different in other countries, and Vi decided that she had misunderstood Zoe's gestures and the monsieur's response.

Comforted by these thoughts, Vi fell asleep almost as soon as she turned out her light. She'd completely forgotten the crumpled envelope that lay on her dressing table.

Shocking News

Because the LORD revealed their plot to me, I knew it, for at that time he showed me what they were doing.

JEREMIAH 11:18

Shocking News

*V*i had decided that they would all go to the Polo Grounds that day. Located just north of Central Park, it was the site of many of the city's popular sporting competitions. Then Mr. Meriweather would drive them farther north, to Harlem Heights, to see The Grange, which had been the summer home of Alexander Hamilton. Vi thought Zoe would enjoy the historic old house and its grove of thirteen trees planted in honor of the nation's thirteen original states.

When Vi presented her plan over breakfast, Zoe had agreed to it eagerly. "It will be a history lesson for me," Zoe said. "I do not know nearly as much as I should about the lives of the people who founded my country. Today I shall learn about Alexander Hamilton."

So they returned to the suite to prepare for their excursion. Vi was searching for her guidebook on her dressing table when her eyes fell on the envelope. For several seconds, she couldn't think what it was. Then she remembered meeting the hotel manager in the lobby the previous afternoon and his giving her a letter. In her anxiety about Zoe, she had paid it no attention, crumpling it in her hand and tossing it onto the table.

Now she smoothed the envelope, and immediately she saw that the return address was her brother's. She opened it quickly, and as she read, her brow furrowed in worry.

It was a short letter. Ed announced that he was coming to New York. He would arrive that very day, on the afternoon train. He apologized for not alerting her sooner, but he said that his trip was a last-minute decision. Then he wrote:

Violet's Turning Point

For some reason, what you said about your new acquaintance "Monsieur Alphonse" bothered me. I can't tell you why. I just had a feeling. So I decided to do some investigating. My visit to you is the result of what I've learned. I do not want to write of it, but I will explain when I see you.

Until then, I do not want you or any of the others to see this man again. Trust me on this, little sister. I'm not trying to dictate to you. I have very good reasons for this warning.

For a moment, she was confused by Ed's letter, for he could not yet have received her request for his help. Then she realized that their letters had crossed in the mail. His suspicions had been raised by a casual mention of the monsieur in one of her earlier letters.

Vi sat down heavily on her bed. Her shoulders sagged as if a heavy weight had just been laid on her back. For the last few days, she seemed to have been living on a seesaw. Up one minute and down the next. What was true, and what was false? Of course, she trusted Ed, and he would be glad to know that she had already determined not to see Monsieur Alphonse again. But what had Ed learned that compelled him to rush to New York? Was the suave Frenchman more dangerous than she imagined? All sorts of wild ideas assaulted her mind, and she struggled to control them.

"It is good to wait quietly," she said, reminding herself of the verses that had comforted her the night before. "You've done everything you can for the present," she said aloud. "There's no cause to upset Zoe or even Mrs. O'Flaherty before you hear what Ed has learned. Now, brush your hair and concentrate on the interesting day ahead. Ed will be at the hotel when we return. Then we will know what is really going on."

She went back to the dressing table and began brushing her hair. Looking into the mirror, she commanded herself out loud, "Smile! 'The LORD is good to those whose hope is in him.' Nothing has happened that cannot be remedied. And with God's blessing, nothing shall."

⁓

Vi informed Zoe and Mrs. O'Flaherty about Ed's impending arrival, and Zoe received the news with her usual good cheer. Before leaving the hotel, Vi reserved a room for her brother and wrote a quick note, telling Ed where they would be and when they would return. She left the note at the hotel desk, asking the clerk to give it to her brother the moment he arrived.

Though Ed's letter puzzled her, Vi again warned herself against jumping to conclusions and determined to keep her worries at bay. She enjoyed herself as they watched the lacrosse players practicing at the Polo Grounds and was charmed by the old country home of Alexander Hamilton. She and Zoe both delved into the guide book for more information about New York's colonial history. They began to plan their excursion for the next day—a visit to Wall Street, where George Washington had delivered his inaugural speech as the first President of the United States, and then to St. Paul's Chapel on Broadway, where Washington had worshipped.

When they returned to the hotel, Ed was waiting. He gave no sign of the real purpose of his visit as he greeted

Violet's Turning Point

Zoe and Mrs. O'Flaherty. They all talked for awhile about the day's activities. Zoe also told Ed about how nice Mr. and Mrs. Despard had been to her, but she made no mention of Monsieur Alphonse. They decided to dine that evening at the restaurant where Ed had taken them on his last night in New York.

Then he took his leave, saying that he still needed to unpack. He asked Vi to come with him, as he had a bit of "family news" for her.

Once in his room, he took some papers from his travel case and said, "I still don't know what made me suspicious of the man, Vi, but I was. So I called on a lawyer—a friend from school who has his own practice. I told him that I needed information on this Monsieur Francois Alphonse, and I needed it urgently. My friend's father is a high official with the government in Washington, so he has excellent contacts. We spent a small fortune in telegraph messages back and forth, but it was worth it."

"What did you learn?" Vi asked anxiously.

"Nothing," Ed said, but he did not intend his reply as a joke. "There was nothing to learn," Ed went on, "because as far as can be determined, there is no Monsieur Francois Alphonse, art dealer from Paris."

Vi's eyes were wide with shock. "But we've met him," she said. "He is staying with the Despards."

"You met a man who calls himself by that name," Ed said as he ruffled the papers in his hand, "but there is no record of him anywhere. No identification papers. No record with any of the ship companies of anyone by that name traveling from France to the United States in the past three months. My friend talked to a number of art collectors, and no one had heard of Monsieur Alphonse. Vi, he is a fake. I believe that the Despards have been taken in by this charlatan, and I have come to warn them."

"They are not the only ones who have been led astray," Vi said with downcast eyes.

"Oh, I know you were fooled," Ed said offhandedly, "and that's why I warned you not to see him again. But clearly the Despards and their wealthy friends are the target of whatever scheme he has planned."

Vi looked up, and Ed read the worry in her face.

"I wrote you just yesterday," she began, "but you couldn't have gotten my letter in time. Now I must tell you what has happened and what we suspect. If Monsieur Alphonse is truly a charlatan, I believe that his target is Zoe."

Now it was Ed who was shocked. He sank down on the bed and stared at his sister.

Vi spoke calmly as she told him all that had occurred — their first meeting with the monsieur, Zoe's frequent contacts with him at the Despards', the conversation overheard by Mrs. Despard and her concern, and what Vi herself had seen the day before.

"I blame myself," she concluded. "Mrs. O'Flaherty and I were so involved with Aunt Louise and Virginia at first. Then I devoted so much of my time to Dr. Frazier's clinic. I just wasn't thinking about my responsibility to Zoe."

By this point, Ed was on his feet again and pacing the floor.

"Have you talked to Zoe?" he asked.

"Not yet," she answered. "Mrs. O'Flaherty and I decided that we wouldn't let her have any opportunity to see the man. But we had no real evidence of anything, Ed. We couldn't violate Zoe's trust."

Ed went to his sister and put his hand on her shoulder. "Don't blame yourself," he said gently. "The man is obviously

a skillful trickster. If Chris Despard could be taken in, anyone could. But we have to act now. We have to talk to Zoe
and tell her what we know."

"Don't be angry with her," Vi pleaded.

"I'm not," Ed replied. He rubbed his moustache and said,
"Really, Vi, I am not angry with her. She has been
deceived—just as Virginia was taken in. Zoe is the victim
of a cunning scheme. But somehow, I think that knowing
will not crush her, as it might many young girls. For all my
criticism of Zoe, I know she has a great deal of strength.
You know what I mean, don't you?"

"Strength of character," Vi said with a little smile. "And
the strength of her faith."

"That's it," Ed said softly, "faith and character."

He walked across the room once more, then turned and
said, "We cannot delay this, Vi. We must tell her now."

Zoe and Mrs. O'Flaherty were both in the sitting room
when Vi and Ed entered. Vi couldn't help but think how
delicate and young her friend was. Too young to be subjected to this kind of hurt. But it had to be done, and Zoe
would endure it with courage. That was her nature.

Zoe, too, was thinking about her friends. She saw immediately the grave looks on Vi's and Ed's faces.

"Zoe, we need to discuss something very serious with
you," Ed began. "It's about Monsieur Alphonse."

Mrs. O'Flaherty started to rise. She guessed what this
conversation would be, and she thought it should be private. But Ed motioned for her to stay seated. Vi went to sit
beside Zoe, and Ed resumed speaking.

Shocking News

As calmly as Vi had been earlier, he revealed all that he now knew about the supposed art dealer. His voice and his words were as kind as possible, but he did not try to conceal anything.

Zoe listened attentively. But to Vi's astonishment, her friend did not seem to be in the least distressed. There were no tears, no hand-wringing. Zoe simply listened, taking in everything Ed said, and even nodding occasionally as if agreeing with his assessments. When Ed finished, she smiled.

"Are you all right?" Vi asked.

Zoe looked at her, and Vi could see something like laughter in her friend's eyes.

"Of course," Zoe said. "Ed had been a very good detective. And you are all real friends to worry so about me. But it is unnecessary."

"What do you mean—unnecessary?" Ed asked. "Don't you understand? He is a charlatan—a cheat—and he has deceived you."

"Much of what you said is true," Zoe replied. "Monsieur Alphonse is not exactly what he seems, but he isn't what you think. I can't tell you everything, but trust me, you will know very soon."

"Know what?" Ed said, and they could all hear the anger rising in his voice. "He has deceived you. He's deceived Vi and Mrs. O. He has deceived the Despards and their friends. How can you continue to believe in him when you know that he is a fraud?"

Zoe ignored Ed's outburst. She turned to Vi and asked the time.

Vi looked at her little watch and said, "Five thirty-five."

"Then you must all wait for another twenty-five minutes," Zoe said with a happy little laugh. "That isn't too long. Then you will learn the truth. And I promise it will make you very happy."

She stood up and went to the door of her room. "Just twenty-five minutes and all will be revealed," she said in an impish tone. Then she disappeared, and the door was shut.

The three people in the sitting room were literally speechless for some time.

Then Ed began pacing and said with exasperation, "Strength of character indeed! That girl is just plain stubborn. Stubborn as an old mule! How can we help her if she refuses to acknowledge the obvious?"

"Maybe she's in shock," Vi said. "Ed, I think that we must return to Ion as quickly as possible. I will write Mamma now, and you can arrange for our tickets. We can leave tomorrow."

"That's probably best," Ed agreed. "Mamma will know how to deal with Zoe. I certainly don't. Did you see how she reacted? It was as if I told her that she'd have to have cake instead of pie for dessert. I tell her that this man is a scoundrel who is after her money, and she smiles at me. She laughs!"

Vi had turned to Mrs. O'Flaherty. She asked, "Don't you think it's best for us to go home, Mrs. O?"

"I guess so," Mrs. O'Flaherty replied uncertainly. She was just as perplexed as Vi and Ed, but she didn't think Zoe was in shock. She had watched the girl closely as Ed had been talking. To her eyes, Zoe had not been surprised by his revelations. It seemed to Mrs. O'Flaherty that Zoe already knew what Ed told her.

Shocking News

"There is something odd here," Mrs. O'Flaherty said.

"That's an understatement," Ed huffed.

Mrs. O'Flaherty paid him no attention, but she asked Vi, "What time is it now?"

Checking her watch again, Vi said, "Fifteen minutes to six."

"Then we have fifteen minutes," Mrs. O'Flaherty said. "Whatever is the answer to this puzzle, Zoe has promised to make it known in fifteen minutes. I think we can give Zoe fifteen minutes."

CHAPTER

15

An Incredible Turn of Events

*Delight yourself in the LORD
and he will give you the
desires of your heart.*

PSALM 37:4

An Incredible Turn of Events

At exactly six o'clock, Zoe waltzed out of her bedroom. She had changed her dress and done her hair, and she looked like a princess. She glanced at each of her three friends and smiled mysteriously, but she said not a word.

Just a moment later, there was a knock at the suite door. Before anyone else could move, Zoe ran and opened it. In walked Monsieur Alphonse, Mr. Biggs, and a distinguished-looking older man whom no one knew.

Working hard not to giggle, Zoe made a series of introductions.

"Ed, I'd like to present Monsieur Alphonse and his associate Mr. Biggs."

Alphonse bowed toward Ed, but Ed was too dumbfounded to move.

Zoe went on, "Vi, Mrs. O, you both know Monsieur Alphonse, but you have not met Signor Luigi Vivante. Signor, this is Miss Travilla, her brother Mr. Edward Travilla, and our dear, dear friend, Mrs. O'Flaherty."

The older man bowed slightly to Ed and Vi, and then he did the most extraordinary thing.

He walked across the room to where Mrs. O'Flaherty sat, bowed deeply from the waist, and said, "I am sincerely glad to meet you, Signora O'Flaherty. It is because of your dedication that I am here."

Mrs. O'Flaherty was, in a word, flabbergasted. She simply could not speak. She raised her hand, and the man took it and lightly kissed it.

A moment passed and Mrs. O'Flaherty finally said, "It is my pleasure, Maestro Vivante."

Violet's Turning Point

Maestro Vivante? A look of utter bewilderment passed between Vi and her brother.

Zoe addressed Monsieur Alphonse, "They know that you are not who you say. But they don't know who you are."

Monsieur Alphonse moved into the room, leaving Mr. Biggs to stand at the door.

"Before I explain myself," the monsieur said, "I must tell you why Maestro Vivante has accompanied me. Mrs. O'Flaherty, you have a most devoted friend in young Zoe. Few of us are so fortunate to know such friendship. Zoe informed me of your history and your husband's. She told me of your hope that someday, Mr. O'Flaherty's music would receive the recognition it deserves. I thought I might be of help. I knew that an old friend of mine, the Maestro, was in New York, and I suggested that he would be just the person to evaluate your husband's compositions. But first I wanted to meet you. Do you remember the afternoon when I arrived here uninvited and you entertained me over tea? Your graciousness to me, your intelligent conversation, and your affection for Zoe convinced me of your sincerity and your good judgment. I told Mr. Biggs that day that I had met a truly remarkable lady who deserved our assistance."

Mrs. O'Flaherty's sapphire-blue eyes were glowing. "But how . . . ?" she asked.

Zoe ran to her side and sat down on the floor at her feet. "Oh, please forgive me, Mrs. O!" she exclaimed. "I gave the music to the monsieur, and he gave it to Maestro Vivante. I knew you kept it in your old valise, and I borrowed it one morning when you were caring for Virginia. I couldn't tell you then. I didn't want you to be disappointed. I had to know what the Maestro said before I told you. I'm so sorry

188

to have kept it a secret, but I didn't want you to be hurt if—if . . ."

Mrs. O'Flaherty reached forward and softly caressed the girl's blonde hair. In a voice trembling with emotion, she said, "I cannot believe that you even remembered my story. There is nothing to forgive, my dear, dear child."

Maestro Vivante spoke next. His accent was Italian though his English was very good. "My old friend brought the music to me, and I agreed to look at it. I admit that I was not hopeful. As an orchestra conductor of some renown, I often receive the works of struggling composers. I am always on—how do you say?—the lookout for new talent. Sadly, most of what I see is not so good. But your husband, Signora O'Flaherty, he had genius. His work has great originality. It was too original, I imagine, for his time."

Mrs. O'Flaherty nodded but said nothing.

The Maestro's voice became very soft as he continued, "Your husband dreamed music of a new kind, and you have kept his dream alive for many years. Now I hope to make it come true. This fall, I will conduct a season for the New York Symphony. I had already determined the program of music, but I hope to make an alteration. I am here to ask for your permission, Signora, to debut Ian O'Flaherty's 'Irish Rhapsody' at the symphony's first performance in the autumn. It would give me the greatest honor to introduce the world to his name and his work. I predict that it will be but the beginning of many performances of his entire repertoire."

Tears were rolling down Mrs. O'Flaherty's weathered cheeks as she said, "You will make my dream come true, Maestro. You have not only my permission, but my deepest gratitude."

Violet's Turning Point

"Splendid!" the Maestro proclaimed. "Now I have one additional request. You know this work better than anyone alive, and I understand from Signorina Zoe that you are also a talented musician. You could be of great help to me in interpreting the rhapsody as your husband intended it to be performed. My wife and I would like you to stay with us here in New York." Then he added with a smile, "I warn you that I shall put you to work, if you can accept my invitation."

Mrs. O'Flaherty looked questioningly at Vi and Ed.

"Oh, you must stay, Mrs. O!" Vi exclaimed.

Ed nodded in agreement, and Mrs. O'Flaherty accepted with a glorious grin and more tears.

"Then it is done," the Maestro said, clapping his hands together gleefully. "Now I must leave, but I will come again tomorrow if that is acceptable. We have many details to consider. Oh, yes, I have all the music, and I am having it copied. I will return your husband's originals to you as soon as the transcriptions are complete. They are treasures, Signora."

"They are the treasures of my heart," she said.

"Then I shall see you tomorrow," he said, bowing again. He turned to Zoe. "I hope to see you too, Signorina. You made all this possible, you know. What an exceptional young lady you are."

Turning to the others, he expressed his pleasure at meeting Vi and Ed. Then he said to the monsieur, "We are expecting you for dinner tomorrow night, Francois. I hope that this mad masquerade of yours will be over by then."

"It will," the Frenchman said, "at least for the most part."

With another quick bow, the Maestro was gone.

"Did that really happen?" Mrs. O'Flaherty was asking of no one in particular.

"It is as real as the beauty of your husband's music, Madam," replied Monsieur Alphonse.

"You were right all along, Mrs. O!" Zoe cried happily. "All those years that you believed, you were right. And everything is real!"

"Not everything," Ed said. He looked directly at the monsieur and demanded, "Who are you?"

Without a moment's hesitation, the monsieur replied, "My name is Francois Alphonse Lecroix du Signorey. There are several more names before the Lecroix, but I forget them."

"He is the Count du Signorey, and he's a very important diplomat from France," Zoe burst out. "He is here *incognito*. That means in disguise. That's why we know him as Monsieur Alphonse."

"Zoe, I've told you many times that my country is a republic," the Frenchman said with an indulgent smile, "and my family no longer carries a title. I am simply Monsieur Lecroix, for the moment."

In spite of herself, Vi had let out a little gasp. "That explains a great deal," she said, "though hardly everything. I think I need to sit down before you tell us the whole story." All that had transpired in the last few minutes had left Vi feeling almost light-headed. She motioned Monsieur Lecroix to a comfortable seat, then took a place on the sofa for herself. Ed joined her, and Vi noticed that his hands shook slightly. She was glad to see that she was not the only one who felt unnerved.

Remembering her manners, Vi asked Mr. Biggs to join them, but the man in brown shook his head and remained stationed by the door.

Violet's Turning Point

"I am sorry to have misled you all," Monsieur Lecroix said, "but it was necessary. I am afraid that I must ask you to observe the secrecy for a few more days. You see, I am to be the new ambassador of my government to yours. It will be announced early next week, after my return to Washington. And then I shall be Ambassador Lecroix. But before taking the post, I wanted to see your country for myself—not as an ambassador but as an ordinary businessman. So I became Monsieur Alphonse, art dealer. I have been to a number of places—Memphis, St. Louis, Chicago, Boston—and New York is my last stop. Your government was not happy about my journey, but they agreed as long as I was accompanied by an agent of the law. That is Mr. Biggs, who is in fact a retired major in your Army, and he has guarded my every move. His usual assignment is to the President, so I have been exceedingly well protected."

"But do the Despards know your real identity?" Ed asked.

"No, but I shall tell them tomorrow," the monsieur replied. He looked at Mrs. O'Flaherty and said, "I hope you will forgive my role in Miss Zoe's little deception. I'm afraid that it was I who suggested keeping it secret until we had the Maestro's judgment."

"I'm not fond of secrets, but I am even less fond of building up false hopes. I would likely have done the same in the circumstances. I have no need to forgive what has brought me so much happiness, sir," Mrs. O'Flaherty said graciously. "Zoe, on the other hand, seems to thrive on secrets," she added, smiling down at the happy girl at her feet.

"I wanted to tell," Zoe protested. "But I just couldn't. I was so afraid that the Maestro might not see the greatness of Mr. O'Flaherty's music. You always said it was ahead of its time, and I was afraid the music might be ahead of him. But when we went to the Maestro's studio yesterday, he played part of the rhapsody for us, and I just knew how wonderful it was."

"Is his studio near here?" Vi asked.

"Just a couple of blocks down this street," Zoe said. "I met Monsieur Lecroix there when I went for my walk yesterday, and we all decided to tell you everything tonight. The Maestro insisted that he speak to Mrs. O personally."

"I see," Vi sighed, and at last she did see.

"But why did you ask Monsieur Lecroix for help?" Ed wanted to know. "It was very forward to request such a thing of someone you'd never met."

"But I did know him!" Zoe laughed. "He was a friend of my father, and I had seen him many times in Paris. He recognized me that first time we saw him at the Despards'."

"I asked her not to tell anyone," Monsieur Lecroix added. "If my true identity became known, I would be forced to end my trip. But now I am most anxious to return to Washington. I am missing my family a great deal."

"Family?" Vi said without thinking.

"My wife and children. I have two rowdy sons and an adorable baby daughter," he replied with obvious pride. "They will be joining me at the embassy next week. I have learned much about the United States in my travels, but I have learned something even more important. My home on earth can be anywhere so long as my family is with me."

He said this last with a shy smile that none of them had seen before. Vi thought, *This is the real man—the loving husband and father. How quick I was to misjudge. What a terrible mistake I almost made.*

Monsieur Lecroix was looking at each of them in turn, and his eyes twinkled in a way that reminded Vi of her own

Papa. Smiling broadly, he said, "For my deception, I beg you to let me make a small amends. I would like to host you this evening at dinner. We will have a celebration. We shall celebrate the beauty of great music, the loyalty of loving friends, and"—he nodded at Zoe—"the freeing power of the truth."

They all agreed, and it was decided that they would dine at the restaurant where Vi had already made reservations.

"There is just one favor I must ask," the gentleman said. "If you please, for now I am still Monsieur Francois Alphonse, the art dealer from Paris."

~

It was nearing midnight, but Vi was still awake. She sat up in bed, a little writing desk balanced on her lap. She was composing a letter to her mother—a very different letter from the one she had expected to write before Monsieur Lecroix's and Maestro Vivante's visit.

The hotel was quiet, and the sounds from the street seemed very far away. A gentle breeze blew through her open window. After such a day, Vi could almost feel her body relaxing. It had been many days since she had felt so calm.

A little earlier, she'd had a long talk with her Heavenly Father, telling Him of her fears and asking for His forgiveness for her misjudgments. She asked for His help as she struggled to understand the true meaning of responsibility for others.

Lord, so much has happened on this trip, and I see now that You have been teaching me all along about responsibility and trust. You saved me from making a dreadful mistake about Monsieur Lecroix and dear, dear Zoe. Thank You for Your faithfulness and merciful goodness in my life, Lord. Thank You for Your patience with me when I struggle with my own impatience. And thank You for fulfilling the dream that Mrs. O has carried for so very long, for she had truly waited quietly and never abandoned hope.

As Vi prayed, she became aware of a powerful feeling of renewal as her Heavenly Father lightened her heart. *It is good to hope in You, O Lord.*

It was in this spirit of quiet joyfulness that Vi had begun her letter to her mother, and the story of all that had taken place in the past few days seemed to flow from her pen.

Everyone else had been in bed for at least an hour—or so Vi thought. She was writing away when she heard her doorknob turn. Looking up, she saw Zoe peeking in.

"Your lamp was still lit," Zoe said a little shyly.

"I'm writing to Mamma," Vi replied. "But I can finish in the morning. Come in."

Zoe approached the bed, saying, "I had to tell you again how sorry I am for not being open with you. I didn't think I was being untruthful, but I was. I was hiding something, and that's as bad as a lie."

"It can be," Vi said, "even when the intent is to do good. I understand your not telling Mrs. O. But really, Zoe, you should have confided in me. It would have saved everyone a great deal of worry."

Zoe hung her head and sighed, "I know that now. But you were so busy with your aunt and your cousin and then at the clinic. What you've done for others seems so important. I didn't want to bother you. Until you told me at dinner how concerned you were, I never thought about how others might regard my little secret. I just wanted to do something good for Mrs. O and to make an adventure of it."

"Well, I made mistakes, too," Vi admitted. "I should have talked to you. I thought that confronting you with my suspicions would make you think that I didn't trust you. But I understand now that I showed lack of trust by *not* speaking to you directly. If I'd been open, everything would have been straightened out. But as it was, I jumped to conclusions that were all wrong, and I'm very sorry, Zoe."

Zoe sat down on the bed and sighed, "I suppose I must apologize to Ed. Even when everything was explained tonight, I could tell that he was mad at me."

"Yes, I think you should apologize to him," Vi said. "But I don't think he is really angry with you. I think that he's upset with himself. He did as I did—jumping to hasty conclusions and investigating Monsieur Alphonse—I mean, Lecroix. So I think that in his heart, Ed's upset with himself. He had an experience many years ago that taught him to consider the consequences of his actions. When he acts impetuously—as we all do sometimes—it makes him feel foolish."

"Thinking before we act—that's a lesson for everybody," Zoe said, "especially me. Everything turned out all right this time, but it might not have. Oh, dear, I could have caused ever so much trouble for the Count—Monsieur Lecroix. What if people really thought he was some kind of fortune hunter? Did you really believe I would elope with him or anybody?"

Vi thought for a moment. She said, "To be honest, Zoe, I did and I didn't. I really do trust you, but we're both still young, and neither of us knows as much as we think we do."

Zoe laughed softly. "That's the truth," she said. "Maybe God made all this happen so we could learn to be wiser in our choices."

"I believe He did," Vi said. "I have a dear cousin who told me something wonderful. She said that every day we are growing toward God. She said that growing up is a wonderful gift as long as our hearts are open to Him and we are willing to learn the lessons He teaches us. She said that being wise means recognizing our mistakes and learning from them."

"Well, I've learned that keeping secrets can be harmful, even when the secrets are good," Zoe said.

"Ed would say that it's a question of thinking ahead and considering the possibilities," Vi said. "There are times when we can keep secrets, if telling something would bring harm to someone else. Then there are little secrets, like what one is going to give a friend for a birthday present. I don't want to give those up, do you?"

"Oh, no," Zoe replied quickly. "Presents are grand surprises, aren't they? I mean, they bring happiness to someone you care about."

Vi agreed. She said, "If you apologize to Ed, that would be like a present for him, and for you, too. It would clear the air between you, and you'd both feel better."

"I'll do it first thing," Zoe said with conviction. "Is he returning to the University tomorrow?"

"He got permission from his professors to take a week away from his studies, so he will be staying until Sunday," Vi said. "He wants to help Mrs. O move to the home of Maestro Vivante and his wife. And he plans to see you and me off on our trip home. He telegraphed Mamma tonight to tell her of the day and time of our return and promising to get us safely aboard our train. With a little persuading, he's agreed that I'm old enough to be your chaperone," she added with a smile. "It will be strange to travel without

Mrs. O, but I'm so happy for her. All those years, she never lost faith."

"It's wonderful, isn't it?" Zoe said in a dreamy way. "I think Mrs. O is the most romantic person I know. To love someone so much that you never have any doubts—that's the kind of marriage I want."

Vi threw up her hands and laughed. "After the week we've just had, I don't want to think about your getting married for a long, long time."

"I still have an awful lot to learn before I could marry anyone," Zoe smiled. "I'm just sixteen, you know."

She stood to go, but she added with a wink, "You are much older than I. You're eighteen, and that's not a girl anymore. A lady of your years needs her beauty rest, doesn't she? So go to sleep now, old lady Vi."

Vi laughed as her friend swept out of the room. Then she put away her writing things and turned out her light. Settling into her pillow, she reflected on Zoe's joking words: "not a girl anymore." Vi wondered what it was that made her an adult. She'd had her birthday a couple of weeks before, but everyone had been so concerned about Virginia and the baby that it had passed without any fanfare. Was she any wiser now that she was older?

Then she had a thought: Had her mother intended this time in New York to be something more than a holiday? Had her beloved Mamma given her this time to experience what it was to be a responsible adult on her own? To make decisions that affected others as much as herself?

Mamma couldn't have known that I'd meet Dr. Frazier or learn so much about what it really means to serve others as Amelia does. She couldn't have known about Monsieur Lecroix or the Maestro. Then Vi smiled to herself. *But she would know that a month in*

An Incredible Turn of Events

New York would bring some new adventure into my life, something that would challenge me. If Mamma had been with us, she would have handled everything so much better than I have. But that's not the point, is it? She wanted this to be my time to learn and grow. She pushed me out of the nest so that I might fly. That was her birthday present to me — the chance to test my wings.

"I have much to tell you about my flight, Mamma," she said aloud in the darkness. "It has been turbulent, but at least I did not fall. Despite my mistakes — or maybe because of them — I feel stronger, and my next flight will take me a little farther and higher. And I won't be afraid, because I know God holds me in His hand."

CHAPTER

16

A Last Surprise

Stand at the crossroads and look; ask for the ancient paths, ask where the good way is, and walk in it.

JEREMIAH 6:16

A Last Surprise

*T*he final days of the New York holiday were an exciting whirl of activity for everyone. First and foremost was the move of Mrs. O'Flaherty. Not that she had much to move. But Zoe insisted that Mrs. O needed new clothes for her new position, and Vi had to agree. So back they went to the shops and the dressmakers. Somehow, the girls even made time for a bit more sightseeing, with Ed joining them.

Mrs. O'Flaherty had several meetings with Maestro Vivante, and Ed insisted that she meet with Mr. Phillips. She would need a good lawyer to represent her interests and protect her husband's works.

Vi could not leave without visiting Dr. Frazier and the clinic again, and on this occasion Zoe asked to go with her. Dr. Frazier made it clear to Vi that she would do whatever she could to help with Vi's mission plans. And she had some good news—the boy who had been injured at the laundry had returned home to his grandmother. When he had his strength back, he would be going to school, and arrangements had been made for his grandmother to receive a generous pension to support them both.

"Dr. Frazier didn't say where that pension came from," Zoe observed as she and Vi left the clinic, "but I think I know."

"I think I do as well," Vi said, "though I doubt she'd admit that she is the boy's benefactor. She keeps her light hidden under a basket, but still it shines forth for all to see."

"I know now why you needed to come to the clinic," Zoe said. "Dr. Frazier's work is like a beacon for you, isn't it?"

Violet's Turning Point

"That's true," Vi said. "She has shown me that it's not enough to have a dream or a sense of calling. She taught me how important it is to have perspective. If I want to serve others, I have to be practical and realistic. Helping with the children at the clinic has taught me so much about listening to other people. I've seen parents bring their little ones in for medical care. But Dr. Frazier takes time to talk with all the children themselves and learn about them. Lots of times they aren't sick, but they need nourishing food or warm clothes. Dr. Frazier is able to send them to some of the churches that provide meals or the mission shelters that offer clothing. She says that being practical often means knowing when she can't help but other people can. What she's done for the boy, Michael, and his grandmother comes from her heart. But there are thousands of children like him, and Amelia can't support all of them. She says that being realistic means using common sense and not trying to do everything by oneself. She told me that to help others often requires asking for help."

"Do you think I might be able to help you? When you have your own mission?" Zoe asked a little hesitantly. "I just know you will have one someday, Vi, just as Mrs. O finally has her dream, and I want to help you. I may seem like a featherbrain sometimes, but I can be practical when it's important."

"I know that I can always use your help," Vi replied. "And your friendship."

"You'll always have that, Vi, no matter what," Zoe said.

Mr. Meriweather remained their devoted driver, and he was almost embarrassed when Ed presented him with an envelope containing a check for a large amount of money and Vi gave him a basket filled with gifts for each of his children.

A Last Surprise

Mr. Meriweather accepted both, saying, "I'm most appreciative of your generosity. The truth is, it's been a real treat for me to be helpful. I'm going to miss you and your friends, Miss Travilla. Whenever you come back to New York, you tell that hotel manager to let me know. Just tell him that you want Kevin Meriweather to be at your service."

On their final Saturday evening in New York, Vi, Zoe, Mrs. O'Flaherty, and Ed were invited to dine with the Despards. It was to be a private evening, Mrs. Despard said, with no other guests. But she had a surprise in store for them. When they entered the Despards' parlor, there was Monsieur Lecroix!

"He delayed his departure for Washington just to see all of you once more," Mrs. Despard said with delight. "I hope you will forgive me for this one little secret."

"I think we should agree that this will be the last secret," the monsieur said with a hearty laugh.

Vi and Zoe's train was to leave the city at four o'clock and Ed's shortly afterwards, so they had most of their last Sunday in New York to themselves. They attended services at a nearby church, and then strolled back to the hotel through the park. In their suite, Mrs. O'Flaherty had a delicious farewell luncheon awaiting them.

"Mamma planned this trip so you girls could shop and learn about the history of New York," said Ed after he'd asked the blessing and they'd all begun eating. "She didn't expect you to *make* history. But that is what has happened. Thanks to Zoe, the world will soon know the glorious music of a great, modern composer."

Zoe blushed and said, "It's all because of Mrs. O. It was her dedication, as the Maestro said. That's what made everything possible."

"And Monsieur Lecroix," Vi said. "He really is a fine man. Just thinking about how I misjudged him makes me cringe. But I've learned my lesson."

"We've all learned many lessons," Mrs. O'Flaherty said with a grin. "Now let us pledge that we will not forget them."

She raised her water glass, and the others followed her lead. "I propose a toast to truthfulness always among friends," she said.

They clinked their glasses together and laughed in agreement.

"And no more secret missions," Vi added. She looked at Zoe and said, "Remember when you told me that you might be on a secret mission? I thought you were joking, and I said that you could never keep a secret. You proved me wrong, Zoe—you and Monsieur Lecroix and Maestro Vivante."

Zoe's smile vanished, and her blue eyes widened. "Oh, my, I almost forgot my secret mission," she said. "It wasn't what you think, Vi. It was another secret mission altogether."

Mrs. O'Flaherty reached over the table and patted Zoe's hand. "Perhaps now is the time to reveal your surprise, young lady," she said.

Zoe stood up. "It's the perfect time," she said, her smile returning, sunnier than ever. She rushed off to her room, and they all heard the bang of her wardrobe door followed by a great deal of rattling and bumping.

"I'm not sure I can take another surprise," Ed remarked. "What is it this time, Mrs. O? Does she have the entire French Army hidden in her closet?"

A Last Surprise

"Just wait a few more moments," Mrs. O'Flaherty smiled knowingly.

Zoe reappeared. She was carrying a largish, rectangular object in her arms. It was wrapped in pink paper and tied with a purple ribbon.

She came to Vi and spoke as if she were addressing a large ceremonial audience. "As you all know, Vi turned eighteen while we were here," she began. "But everyone was so worried about Virginia and the baby and getting them well that Vi asked Mrs. O and me not to mention her special day, and we didn't. But we couldn't forget it, Vi. And we have a gift for you. It's not just from us, as you will see. So here is our secret mission."

Ed moved Vi's plate and silverware aside, and Zoe laid the package on the table. Vi stood and untied the purple ribbon. She lifted off the wrapping paper and gazed in astonishment at her present.

It was a painting in a handsome gold frame.

"It's the *piazza*!" Vi exclaimed. "It's the plaza in Rome. Oh, Ed, it's where Zoe and I found little Alberto Constanza! And of course, I know the artist. This is Lester's work. But how?"

"He painted it for you before Mrs. O and I left Rome," Zoe said, bubbling with excitement. "We brought the canvas back with us, and our secret mission was to have it framed for your eighteenth birthday. Remember that day when you were at the clinic and Monsieur Lecroix visited Mrs. O'Flaherty and me? Mrs. O and I told you that we had a little more shopping to do. You probably thought we were buying something frivolous, but in fact we were getting this picture from the framer, and I've kept it in my wardrobe ever since. We were waiting for the right time to give it to you. So this is our secret mission!"

Violet's Turning Point

Vi could not take her eyes from the painting. "But just look what Lester has done," she said. "The faces of the people! All the people in the plaza are people I know. There's Alberto and his family. And the policeman and the flower vendor. Come and see, Ed! Lester painted himself and Missy sitting with Zoe and Mrs. O at the outdoor café. And there's the sad lady at the hotel—she's sitting just behind them. Everyone is just as I remember. But how did he know?"

"You left your sketchbook at the hotel, and the manager found it," Zoe explained. "The manager gave it to my Papa, and Papa gave it to Missy and Lester. That's what inspired Lester to do the painting."

"He said that you had captured the essence of your Roman adventure in your drawings," Mrs. O'Flaherty noted. "He said that you could look at his painting and your experiences would always be fresh for you."

Vi had to sit down. As the memories came flooding back, she found herself laughing and crying at the same time.

"You're there too, Vi," Ed said. He was looking over her shoulder and pointing. "See? Behind the flower cart. It's you and Grandpapa."

"My Papa is there, too—talking to Dr. Di Marco and Mrs. Warden beside the fountain," Zoe said. "When you see everyone together like that, it's amazing. I mean that so many people crossed paths and influenced each other's lives in just a few weeks."

Vi could barely see for the tears in her eyes. She wiped them away and looked up at Zoe and Mrs. O'Flaherty. "Thank you so, so much," she said. "I have never had such a wonderful gift."

"Maybe someday Lester can paint us all in New York," Zoe said with a happy laugh.

208

"But we will have music to remember New York," Ed said. "The 'Irish Rhapsody' by Ian O'Flaherty will always bring our New York memories back to us." He smiled at Mrs. O'Flaherty.

"And the dresses," Mrs. O'Flaherty said with a grin.

That remark got all their attention. Vi, Zoe, and Ed looked at her in curiosity.

"Just think about it," Mrs. O'Flaherty said. "Think about what has happened in the last month. Think of how God led Vi and Mrs. Conley to Virginia and brought a family together again. Think how His path led you, Vi, to Dr. Frazier. How Ed's friendship with the Despards led us to Monsieur Lecroix. How my casual story about my husband's music struck Zoe's kind heart and made the dream of a lifetime come true. I have never believed in coincidences. I believe in God's guiding hand. He brings us to turning points, and He lets us choose which direction we will take. He guided us all to New York and gave us the opportunities to make choices. Whatever mistakes were made, we have learned from them. But your ultimate choices, my dear young friends, have led to great happiness for others."

"But you said 'dresses,' " Vi remarked in a puzzled tone. "I don't understand what dresses have to do with anything."

"You must remember how it began," Mrs. O'Flaherty said, her eyes dancing with good humor. "Our Zoe needed some new dresses."

"And that brought us to New York and to so many turning points!" Vi exclaimed. "God does move in mysterious ways!"

They all laughed and hugged, but it was Ed who had the last word.

Violet's Turning Point

"Zoe's dresses," he said, shaking his head with amusement. "Well, I have learned another lesson, thanks to you three. I will never again joke about your talk of silks and satins and flounces and bustles."

"Or henhouses?" Vi said teasingly.

"From now on, little sister," he said, "I promise you this. Henhouses are strictly for chickens and not the subject of jesting. I would be a very foolish man to risk offending such witty, wise, and determined women."

Then he stroked his mustache and added, "I can't even imagine what your next adventure will be, ladies, or where it will lead you. But whatever it is, I hope you'll invite me along for the ride."

Will Vi's mission of service succeed?
When danger threatens, who will come to her rescue?
What new adventures lie ahead?

Violet's story continues in:

VIOLET'S BOLD MISSION

Book Four
of the
*A Life of Faith:
Violet Travilla* Series

A Life of Faith: Violet Travilla

With many more to come!

Mission City Press

For more information, write to

Mission City Press at P.O. Box 681913,
Franklin, Tennessee 37068-1913
or visit our Web Site at:

www.alifeoffaith.com

Collect all of our Elsie products!

A Life of Faith: Elsie Dinsmore

* Now Available as a Dramatized Audiobook!

Collect all of our Millie products!

A Life of Faith: Millie Keith Series

* Now Available as a Dramatized Audiobook!

Check out
www.alifeoffaith.com!

- Get news about Violet, Elsie & Millie

- Find out more about the 19th century world they live in

- Learn to live a life of faith like they do

- Learn how they overcome the difficulties we all face in life

- Find out about Violet, Elsie & Millie products

- Join our girls' club

A Life of Faith® Books
It's Like Having a Best Friend From Another Time!